Catfish Joe & Double, Double, Toil, & Trouble

Two Novellas

CAROL ANN

iUniverse, Inc.
New York Bloomington

Catfish Joe & Double, Double, Toil, & Trouble
Two Novellas

This is a work of fiction. All of the characters, names, incidents, organizations, and dialogue in this novel are either the products of the author's imagination or are used fictitiously.

iUniverse books may be ordered through booksellers or by contacting:

iUniverse
1663 Liberty Drive
Bloomington, IN 47403
www.iuniverse.com
1-800-Authors (1-800-288-4677)

ISBN: 978-1-4502-2709-4 (sc)
ISBN: 978-1-4502-2710-0 (ebk)

Printed in the United States of America

iUniverse rev. date: 5/21/2010

CATFISH JOE AND THE YOUNGBLOOD

"What the fuck's the matter with you, you old fuck?" You lookin' at me?" said the Gansta Boy in his low slung, Blue jean pants and ass turned around red baseball cap.

"I aint be lookin' at you, Boy. I done seen it all." replied Catfish Joe.

"You aint got nothin' to give me, motherfucker?" asked Bad Boy.

"I aint got shit for you, Boy. Spent my whole check on cigarettes and booze," said Catfish Joe.

"You sho' aint spend nothin' on yo' appearance. That's for sho'," snickered Bad Boy, and he further commented,

"You aint got no business drinkin'. Like to give you a heart attack, or the shits at the least. And smokin' aint no damn good neither."

"Where you get yo' medical degree, Boy? Gansta U? And what I got to look good fo? I aint no fancy pimp or nothin'. As fo the drinkin', nothin' but the best fo' old Joe, Fast Ford, (Thunderbird)."

And the old man laughed. There was a rattle in his chest.

"Besides, even Jesus, hisself turned water into wine. You should know that from yo' Bible trainin'."

"What make you think I got Bible trainin.?"asked Bad Boy.

"Everybody get The Word when they's young.You jes' fell off the God train. And you headed straight fo' hell, and the Devil be shovin' his pitch fork straight up yo' young ass.'

"Shut the fuck up, and fork it over.

Or I'll mess you up good, Bitch," Said Bad Boy.
The old man laughed and said, "Boy does I look like
I got me some titties? What you mean, Bitch? " said old Joe.
"Give it up, Motherfucker," said the boy.
"I aint never done that and aint likely to," said old Joe,
and emptied his pockets.
Only pennies fell out.
"See, pennies from heaven, Boy."
Then he had a laugh riot and several spasms of coughing.
"Dang," said the Boy, "Why aint you take yourself to the doctor,
Old Head? You got TB or somethin'?"
"Boy, I got everything known to man and then some.
I aint got no money for no doctoring," replied old Joe.
"If I be a gnat's ass from Old Man Death,
What make you think I want to go on livin'?"
I done it all, Boy," said old Joe.
"You fucked up in the head, old man.
Aint nobody who done everything," said Gansta Boy.
"Well, you aint never known ol' Catfish Joe," he said.
"My name's Tyrone. Why yo' name be Catfish Joe?" said the Boy.
"I fishes the river fo' catfish. Do that explain my name
Good enough fo' you?" said the old man.
"What else you eat?" asked Tyrone.
"This and that," replied old Joe.
"Boy, why you be up in my bidness?"
Does I look like the fuckin' encyclopedia or somethin'?"
"You look like somethin' else entirely, Old Man,
But I aint sayin'", said Tyrone.
"How you get yosef' in a fucking mess like this?"
"Who say I be bad off? I lives off the land like Tarzan.
You want my goddamn life story, Boy?" he asked.
"Why you aint call me Tyrone, Mr. Joe. I done give you
my name."

"Sorry," replied old Joe. "It's nothin' on you. I just aint used to people givin' me they Christian names no mo'. Tyrone, you got some time to spend?"

"All the time in the world, Mr. Joe," he replied.

"Okay I be tellin' ya my story. One time when I was young, I was rich as Croesus. I had me six fine, fat, juicy Bitches and they wasn't no ho's neither. None of my womens had to work. Just lay back, fuck, and look pretty, that's all. And I had me a big, giant Mansion with twenty servants. They was all white, you see. I figured, why not fuck 'whitie" cuz he done fuck me royally Fo' so long. Tyrone, I tell ya it was heaven."

"Tell me about the Bitches, Mr. Joe," asked Tyrone.

"Oh, they was the finest pussy this side of Mississippi. Big, black, and juicy as goddamn Georgia peaches. They was horny as cats in heat, too. They loved the hell, out of they ol' Daddy Joe. I done it all with them. The suckin'. The fuckin'. Old Joe know what to do wif a woman. Then when I done give one money to buy a pretty dress, Another bitch find out and she be jealous like ol' Daddy Don't love her as much as the first Bitch. Then I gives her money and she go get an even better dress. them Bitches was a trip. I tell ya, Tyrone."

"And what about yo' mansion", asked Tyrone.

"Oh, boy, it was splendid. Just splendid. Twenty six rooms, all done in white, white furniture, white shag carpets. The Works! I even had me some Elvis paintings and bull fighter paintings on black velvet. I likes art. It was real class, I tell ya' I also had me a turquoise Cadillac with zebra upholstery. Shit, them were the days, Tyrone."

The old man's eyes misted over.

"Mr. Joe," said Tyrone, "How you gone tell me you wasn't no pimp, Where you git' the money!"

"Tyrone," he replied, "I be a God fearin' man. I wasn't never no pimp. They's evil Bastards. Goin' straight to Hell fo' damn sure."

"Then where'd you git' the money?" asked the Boy.

"Well I be tellin' ya' shortly, Just you hold yo' damn horses. Listen, Tyrone, when you was little did you believe in Santy Claus and the Easter Bunny, and witches, and shit?" asked old Joe.

"Sho', Mr. Joe," replied Tyrone.

"Well, I got somethin' kind of weird to tell ya'. But I wants to tell ya' I ain't no goddamned head case. Tyrone, I had me this old, brown mule, the name of Sugar. And when I would hold up her tail and it was time to go, she shat diamonds. Big, beautiful diamonds, and nothin' else. Then the old Bitch died on me, and I didn't have nothin' no mo'.

Lost the mansion and the Bitches, too. Aint no woman gonna fuck with no po' ass man. You, believe me, son?"

Tyrone paused and looked directly at old Joe.

"Sho', I believes ya, Mr. Joe. It was some damned Bad Ass Luck. Mr. Joe, why you aint come home with me for dinner? ham, grits, greens and biscuits. You like peach cobbler? Mr. Joe," said Tyrone.

Mr. Joe replied, "Boy, you don't know me like that. How I know You aint poison me, or some shit?"

Then Tyrone smiled, and said, "My gram's a God fearin', high yella Gal and she got ass for miles and she aint had none in twenty years. And she fine, Mr. Joe. Real fine.

"Boy, why you aint tell me this befo'? Give me my cane and let's git to steppin'," said old Joe.

And they walked off into the sunset,

And Tyrone turned to the old man, and said, "See, Mr. Joe, I do know you like that."

And he smiled real hard like he was the goddamned morning sun.

ETTA

Tyrone and Mr. Joe walked the long black road in the dark moonless night and Mr. Joe remarked, “Dang, them crickets is a chirpin’ away. They always happy cuz they got no sense.”

“Is you always happy, Mr. Joe?” asked Tyrone.

“Sho’ I is boy. I aint got no sense neither,” And they both laughed.

“Lookit them corn stalks in the dark, Tyrone. Aint they look like some weird kind of alien in the darkness?”

“Sho’ do, Mr. Joe. This here piece be’s part of our land, Mr. Joe. Grams and me works it together. I picks up the eggs, milks the cow and feeds the hogs and other animals. Grams runs the husking machine and cooks, and sews, and shit. Mebbe she find somethin’ fo you, Mr. Joe.”

“I done farm work befo’. Mebbe this be good fo’ everybody some kind of way. What kind of woman yo’ grams be, Tyrone?”

“She like dick but she aint no ho’. And if you done her real wrong she might jes’ stick ya and bury yo’ ass in the lower forty,” replied Tyrone.

“That be good to know, Tyrone. I gone behave all mannerful and considrit’ like Colonel Saunders.”

“Don’ behave like no damn white man, Mr. Joe. The she gone cut you fo’ sho’,” warned Tyrone.

“That also be good to know, Tyrone. I use the brain what God gave me and lets nature takes its course. Ol’ Joe good with womins. Damn Good.”

“Is you braggin’ ‘bout yo’ size, Mr. Joe,” asked Tyrone.

"That aint even up fo' discussion, Ty. It take mo' than jes' size to please a woman. If that be all it took all it took, all our womins be out in the pasture ballin' the mules and horses all the damn time!"

"That be somethin' I aint care to 'magine," replied Tyrone.

"You don' worry 'bout Ol' Joe. I be a damn site smarter than I looks."

"That be good to know," replied Tyrone.

"Look boy, this be the crossroads where Robert Johnson done sold his soul to the devil to git' his talent!" exclaimed Mr. Joe.

"Who he?" asked Tyrone.

"He be an old time blues singer, Ty. Yo' grams probly' know him."

"I don' know them ol' guys. They corny, Mr. Joe," replied Ty.

"You is a knucklehead, boy. And they aint no known cure fo' that."

"Mr. Joe, how you gone sell yo' soul to the devil. He aint no real type person. Do he make house calls like a dang doctor?"

"You showin' some cogitation, boy. Lookit, Tyrone, they is a battle between the Lord, or the forces of Good, and the Devil, or the forces of Evil every damn day in this world," expounded Mr. Joe.

"Oh, Mr. Joe, that jes' plain corny and things jes' aint that simple. Some people jes' deserves to be fucked over!"

"And how 'bout me, Ty, did I deserve it?" queried Mr. Joe.

"No, you was a mean, old fucker. So's I lef' ya alone," replied Ty.

"So who do deserve it, Ty?" asked Joe.

"Those who aint got no balls, Mr. Joe. They gon' cry, please don' take my money, I needs it to buy food or I needs it fo' my medcine'. Hell, they aint got no self respec'!"

"You think?" replied Mr. Joe.

"They bitches and moans. It make me sick so I fucks 'em over royally. You aint want to show yo' soft side in this world!" intoned Ty.

"And what 'bout me? You aint mess wid Ol' Joe?"

"I could see ya' had class even though ya' looked like a piece of shit. They was jes' somethin' 'bout ya', Mr, Joe."

"God be sittin' on my left shoulder every goddamned day, boy. That what it was. Things do be pretty black and white, Ty. You don' want to fuck wid' the Lord. In Hell, yo' brains done boil in yo' head like some kind of soup, and you can smell yo' own flesh searin'. And worst of all, you sees who you really was not who you thought you was. They runs a big movie of yo' damn life over and over again.

And another thing, Ty, they aint no sex in Hell, only in Heaven. In Hell, they got these real beautiful, red hot woman wearin' black velvet bunny suits and high spiky heals. They too hot to touch and if you let them go down on you they bites it off. They there to remind ya, you aint never gone get no ass again!"

"What about fo' womin?" asked Ty.

"Oh, they got this real good lookin' dude. He be like Favio and rubs up against them and says all this nasty shit to get them all hot and bothered. Only, he gay. Big Time. And they never catches on. That be the torture. Son, you see bad ass people don' know they is evil. They only thinks they is do'in what they gots to do. People does sell they Soul to the Devil every day, Ty. Get yo' young ass together. I aint foolin'."

"Okay, Mr. Joe, you right. Don' git' yerself in a tizzy. We almost there. Now look ahead, Mr. Joe," said Ty.

Mr. Joe saw the orange lights rise out of the mist, a kind of vital brightness in the total blackness of the night. Then he saw Tyrone's house, a white clapboard house with a white picket fence. Purple and yellow pansies lined the walkway and two fresh pies were cooling in the window. A sweetness floated in the air and Mr. Joe's underprivileged belly ached with hunger. There was a welcome mat in the door that proclaimed, "God Bless Our Happy Home."

Ty called out, "Yo. Grams, I bought a guest, and he be hongry. Real hongry. He, my friend, Mr. Joe."

"Well, Ty. Go on wit' yerself and bring 'em in! I can't stands to see nobody hongry! It jes' aint seemly." Her voice was low and melodious like an oboe.

Old Joe stepped gingerly into the room, conscious of any noise his big feet might make. He noted the plainness of the furniture in the room and the hand knitted doilies on the wooden tables. A large print of Jesus was prominently displayed in the living room. His eyes glowed like two golden pieces of topaz. Braid rugs covered the crude, plank floors. Everything had that scrubbed and polished look.

She was standing at the stove stirring her pots and pans, and she did as Tyrone mentioned, have ass for miles. Then she put her utensils down and came over to greet them. When she stood before him, Joe felt as if he had been blasted in the face by a shot gun. Such was her beauty. Pretty is tame like a new born kitten. Beauty is savage. Beauty is sorcery. It paralyzes the heart. Her figure was statuesque like a gigantic Sophia Loren and her waist was tiny and tight. Her eyes were large and almond shaped, the color of a shady pond with a multiplicity of brown specs. Her cheek bones jutted out sharply and her chin and jaw line were firm and well defined. There was a slight cleft in the middle of her chin. Her nostrils flaired slightly giving the aspect of a wild cat. Her mouth was lush and sharply cut like those of women in fashion magazines. A wild mass of light brown, curly hair snaked down the middle of her back. "This woman don't know no mirror," he thought as his eyes wandered over to her well stocked book shelf.

She threw back her head and let out a loud belly laugh.

"You looks like you done seen a ghost, honey. Is you mute? I be Etta and you welcome in my house. Ty aint never brung any of his friends home wid him. I spec' he 'shamed of me!"

"It be my genuine pleasure to meet ya', Miz Etta. I be honored to be in yo' presence. Any place I can wash up?" asked Joe.

"Ty, show Mr. Joe the well, and be mindful of snakes," she said.

"Aint no worry, Miz Etta, I done drove all the snakes out of the Garden of Eden mysef'. Those pies be peach and not apple by any chance?"

"Oh, Mr. Joe, I loves a funny man. I hates them gloomy Guss's who rains on parades!" And she laughed again and Joe thought, "I aint never heard anyone laugh like that."

Then they sat down to a meal in silence for the most part. Tyrone was very grateful for this as muggers do not usually like to discuss their day. The meal was honey cloved ham, candied yams, greens, and rice and red beans, and cornbread. Mr. Joe ate two heaping plates of food and had three pieces of peach cobbler. He could see her silent delight at his appreciation of the meal and he further saw hard questions forming in her clear, still eyes. It was kind of like watching water building up behind a dam, and the hope that it would not overflow.

After dinner, Miz Etta sent Ty to his room to read his Bible. After he left, she said, "Aint no way he gone do that. The dang little bastard!"

Then she asked Mr. Joe if he would have coffee and brandy with her.

And he replied, "You done know me, Miz Etta."

She inquired what his profession was and he told her he was a fisherman at the time but that he was a professional boxer at one time. And she asked why he quit or did he just get too old to do it.

"I quit, Miz Etta, when I was thirty-five cuz I done kilt a man. I saw the light just go out of his eyes. It okay to kill in war cuz you is defendin' yo' country, But to kill fo' recreation or fo' money, that be a sin. I done give my entire purse to his wife but it still wasn't right. I pay every day that I lives fo' what I done. I tries to do God's will."

Miz Etta got up and went around behind him. And he thought, "Good she gone give me a hug."Instead she yanked his hair back severely and put a butcher knife under his chin. "I 'spec you gone do some listenin', Mr. Joe. "I lookin' fo' a man but not in the way you might think. I wants someone to straighten out my Ty. He in wit' the wrong crowd, be floatin' down the river like a winter leaf. The path of least resistance. The devil have that boy in his sway, and he aint smart enough to know it. Mr. Joe, I knows you is a smart man. Stupid people talks all the time. Smart folk, they don' say nothin'. If you say you can't, I gone slit yo' goddamn neck and bury ya' in the lower forty." She then pressed the knife in deeper. "If you aint sincere, I gone find ya' anyway and do the same. To me, it aint no never mind and it won't be the first time I ever done straighten out no goddamned man! Raise yo' right hand if ya thinks ya can do it," said Miz Etta.

Joe slowly raised his hand, and he noticed he had a powerful, insistent, even ludicrous erection. "God don' let her notice or I be a goner fo' sho'" he thought.

"I 'splain further, Mr. Joe, just so's we understands each other. I done tricked twenty goddamned years fo' a fine lookin', big dick, cheatin' ass brother. His smile be like the mornin' sun comin' through the slats in the blinds. And he could make me weep and moan all night long. He aint never give me one dime and I gives him diamond rings, Cadillacs, fancy suits. Any damn thing he want. And he marry me and he tell me I be his Precious Darlin'. Then I catches him wid some lil' boys, not even eleven and I cleans the po' lil' things up good befo' sending them home. And he be lookin' real, real scared and I tell 'em, 'Baby, it aint no thing. I understands. Everybody got they own special thing.' Then I gits' on him and fucks him like hell fire and right when he be comin', I slits his throat wid a straight edge. I watches it spurt 'til it die down. Red be just a lovely, lovely color, Mr. Joe.

"Then I find I be wit child and I comes here and buys this farm. What you got to say to that, Mr. Joe," said Etta as she ran her tongue over her bottom lip.

"Girl, you in fo' the fuckin' of yo' life. You needs a man. What you had was a sissy. Don' give me no sass now. I be in no mood fo' it!"

He spat out each word like a bullet aimed at her heart.

Her big green eyes widened and she threw back her wild head and let out a gigantic belly laugh. Then she grabbed Mr. Joe's big hand and placed it on her ass, leading him up the stairs.

When they got to the top of the stairs, she turned to Mr. Joe, looking deeply into his eyes and said, "Mr. Joe, I hopes ya knows this aint jes' no throw down. I wants a little pieces of yo' heart but not the whole goddamned thing. I aint greedy."

"Baby, you gone git' prime cut. Don' worry."

Then they went into the bed room and Old Joe removed his clothes and lay in the dark with his raw, red cock jutting up like a rocket. He knew she wanted to ride him without a word from her. She let her clothes float to the ground like stray onion peels. In the darkness, she was massive, solid, dangerous, and yearning like the Biblical Lilith. She melted slowly like a hot orchid into the velvety softness of the night. And the room infused with the smell of fresh, ripe nectarines. Mr. Joe found that nature does, indeed abhor a vacuum. Yes, it does.

GO WIT GOD IF HE'LL GO WIT YOU

Catfish Joe was plum beat even though he got a new sleeping bag from Deacon Brown. He wasn't in the habit of accepting charity. Old Joe loved the Lord, and each day when he awoke,
"He said, "Thank you Jesus, for another day, Glory Be."

Old Joe never had much truck with evil, and when he saw it, he looked the other way. But if he saw someone weaker being attacked, or threatened by a bully, he would intervene, stepping between the two. He would draw himself up to his full six foot two, and say, "Jes' what is the problem here?"

Old Joe was a vision of madness with his stiff, gray black hair standing straight up, and his fierce, brown eyes. He was a boxer in his twenties and thirties, and he looked the part. There was a jagged knife scar running down his left cheek, and the putrid piece of evil would see his muscular, corded arms, and thick barrel chest.

And he would get it in his mind, "This crazy, old fucker gone kill me! "If the perpetrator did not just take off running, he would say something like, "My Bad. I was just messin' around. I didn't mean nothin'. And then, he would take off running .

Then Old Joe would laugh, and say.

"That teach him not to fuck wit' the Lord. I ain't say I be the Lord, but he sho' do work through me sometime."

Good shines through even if it isn't polished.

That particular day Old Joe was trying to get some shut eye. Perhaps he was in the wrong place for that, a busy CVS drug store in West Philadelphia.

He had dozed off and was dreaming of The Supremes, in red sequined evening dresses, singing, "You Can't Hurry Love." And Dianna was looking right at him.

"Hey, mister, hey mister," said a little white voice.

And he thought, "Oh, shit why I can't get my damned sleep?"

The he opened his eyes and saw a little blond, blue eyed girl, dressed in pink organza with a rabbit fur coat. She even had little white gloves on like Mickey Mouse.

And, he thought, "This be why folks always thinks angels is white."

"Hey, mister, why are you lying in that sleeping bag on the sidewalk?"

"Well, Lil Sistah', I be waitin' for them to give me the key to the city. When I gets that I 'spec I gets up," he said.

"The keys to the city, like the mayor gives you?"

asked the girl who appeared to be about eight years old.

"Why? she further queried.

"Cuz I be such a swell guy, Baby, replied old Joe. Now ya' lets Ol' Joe ast ya' a few questions. Where yo' mama at and why she done leave ya'?

"Well", replied the child, her eyes tearing up, and she swallowed hard.

"I lost her and mommy's going to be really mad at me."

The tears really started running down her pretty, pale face.

"Hey, hey, Lil Lady aint nothin' that bad to boohoo for. I can see you is good in yo' little heart, and that's all that really matters."

"I lost Roxie when I went to pull up my slip. Mommy told me never let anyone see my undies. It isn't nice. And she got away and wouldn't come back to me when I called," replied the girl. "Roxie was our guard dog and she was keeping me safe while mommy was inside."

"What kind of dog, she be, honey," asked Joe.

"A pit bull," replied the little girl.

"Oh, no she didn't! Leave you with a mean ass dog like that!

You still aint tell what I ast you. Is you mama in the sto'?" asked Joe.

"Yes," replied the child. "She's getting her woman's things and some meds."

"Aint right leavin' you all alone like this. Ol' Joe gone sure straighten her out when she come out. In the mean time, you stay wid' Ol' Joe. Honey if some damn white man drives up in a big van, and asts you to go wid' him to find a lost puppy you tell him no. That you stayin' wid' Mr. Joe. I keeps ya' till yo' mamma comes out, okay?"

"Okay, Mr. Joe," said the child.

"You got a nice, big, pink smile on ya, you know that," said Joe.

"Where do you live, Mr. Joe? And why are you lying here?" asked the child.

"I know you're not waiting for the key to the city. They only give that to rich people," exclaimed the child.

"Honey you done say a mouthful. You is smarter than you looks," replied Joe.

"I skipped a few grades in school," she said, shyly ducking her head.

"Oh, well then," replied the old man," I be out here because the servants is cleaning my mansion. They gits nervous if I be there. They thinks I might go off on them."

"Mr. Joe we got a mansion too. Kind of like the one the Queen of England has. Mommy says not to tell. People might get mad," interjected the child.

"Ol' Joe don't hate nobody, baby. Rich or po'."

He ran his hand lightly over her strawberry blond head.

"What's your mansion like, Mr. Joe?" she asked.

"I spect it be a little bit different than yourn. It be made of milk chocolate and candy canes," he replied.

"Really?" she said.

"Sho', Baby," said Old Joe.

"Mr. Joe, how you keep from eating the chocolate?"

"Will power, Honey, will power," he replied.

"I think you may be playing a joke on me. How do you clean chocolate?" said the child.

"Very carefully," he replied and busted out in gales of laughter, followed by some rather severe coughing spasms.

"My daddy's a doctor, Mr. Joe," she said. "I can give you his card."

She took it out of her little patent leather clutch and it to him.

Joe's eyes misted over for a moment and she caught it.

"That be real, real sweet of you, honey, but I aint sure that Ol' Joe be one of your daddy's kind of clients."

"Daddy helps everyone. He's a very good person," she replied.

"I be sho' he is, honey. What be yo' name?" asked Joe.

"Miranda," she said, tossing her blond mane. "And yours?"

"I be Ol' Catfish Joe. Everybody done know me."

"Why, Catfish?" she asked.

"Lil, Gal, that's cause I be a Fisher of Men."

The girl looked puzzled and said nothing. "I just be kiddin' ya, Gal. Aint nobody gone do what Ol' Joe tell em to do."

"What's a Fisher of Men, Mr. Joe? Do you get them from a lake or something, while they're swimming and just put hooks in their mouths? I think that must be against the law," asserted Miranda.

"Miranda, I don' believe it. Your really don't know, do you?"

"Know what?" asked Miranda.

The Fisher of Men be Jesus Christ, Greatest Man who ever lived.,"replied Joe.

"Who's he?" asked the child.

"Miranda, baby, you aint had no Bible trainin,'" queried Joe.

"Oh, you mean Christianity. Mom told me someone might say something one day."

"Oh, she did, did she?" stated Joe.

"First of all, Mr. Joe, we don't believe in the Bible. It's just a nice story like Goldilocks and the Three Bears."

"Oh she say that, do she. I feel my pressure rising," said Joe, placing his hand on his forehead. I be tellin' ya you looks a little like Goldilocks yerself only a damn sight brighter. I can't see you eatin' no bear's food then stayin' around fo' them to beat yo' lil' ass. No sir," said Mr. Joe.

"We believe in the Goddess," said Miranda.

"Who that, Wonder Woman?" asked Joe.

"No, silly, she's Mother Earth," replied Miranda.

"Honey, aint no woman what ever created this earth. Y'al best do the cookin' and somethin' else that I aint sayin'. God created this whole world in seven days.

Mr. Joe further expounded.

"I sees God in all things. Just living is a miracle in itself. I gone tell you the Story of Job cause you needs it. Job was a real God Fearin' man and the Lord, He decide to test his faith and he kick Job's ass fo' days, and he still keep his faith, and his wife say he crazy, but he don' lissen'. And God reward him for his Faith by givin' him everything he want. See. Lil' Gal, life be that way. Sometime you be up: sometime you be down. But you always in the Palm of God's Hand."

Mr. Joe, why can't we talk to him?" asked Miranda.

"He don' do it that way no mo'. You know when you gets a real, sweet thought, Miranda? That be God workin' through you," said Joe.

"Mommy says if you can't see it, or touch it, or hear it, it isn't real." said Miranda.

"Look, Miranda, do you got a heart? Do you got a brain?" said Joe.

"Well, sure I do," she said putting her pretty little hands on her hips.

"Well, you can't see them neither. And what 'bout the air? You can't see it, but without it, you be dead as a squashed June bug," said Mr. Joe.

"Mr. Joe, I'm too little, you're confusing me, and that's not what Mommy says. But, Mr. Joe, I know you're very nice."

"Thank you, Baby, said Joe and his warm eyes glowed like two pieces of obsidian.

Just then Miranda's mother shot out of the store. She had about her the air of a very distraught race horse. Clothed in a short, black Versace suit, she was the very essence of fashion. Her ash blond hair was pulled back severely in a French twist secured by a diamond and silver clasp. Her designer sun glasses had just the right amount of arrogance mixed with entitlement.

"Miranda, why are you talking to this, this, beggar?" she demanded.

"Madam," said Joe, "I aint no Donald Trump but I sho' aint no damn beggar. The Lord will provide for Ol" Joe."

"Where the hell is Roxie?" she snapped.

"I, I lost the dog, mommy. I didn't mean to, and that's Mr. Joe.

He's been watching me so no one bad could get me."

"I just bet he has," said the mother, pulling up her child by one arm.

"Miranda, how many times have I told you not to speak to strange men? Just how difficult is that?"

Then she put her down and put both her hands on the child's cheeks.

"Miranda, look me in the eyes. Did this man touch you or ask you to go anywhere with him?"

"No, mommy, no," said Miranda sobbing, "I was afraid. You didn't come out right away like you usually do and Mr. Joe kept me safe."

"And what do you have to say for yourself, you old bum?"

"And what I got to say, Mrs. Doolittle. Plenty. Does I look like I got me some severed heads in my knap sack. You think I is Ted Bundy, or that other fella', Heidnick. Nosiree, cause they's white men. Aint no black man never hurt no innocent chile!" exclaimed Joe."And where was you, Miss Fancy Pants, leavin' yo' little angel all alone like that?"

"Listen, you ignorant reprobate, do you know who I am?" she fumed.

"No Ma'am and I 'spect you aint know neither. You aint even teach your Lil' Gal about The Word. Who she gonna' call on when she get her little tail in a crack?"

"On me! I'm her mother!" she screamed.

"Oh you is doin' a bang up job of that leavin' yo little angel with a pit bull! Why aint you just use a T-Rex?" spouted Old Joe.

"And furthermo', you done pretend you was helpin' her when what you was doin' was tearin' up her lil' heart. You think you is classy but you aint got no damn heart! See how you is. I bet you don't see at all. You better wake yo ass up befo' you ruin yo precious lil' one! What you gonna' worship on the citadel of the Great Almighty Credit Card?"

Miranda's face was a bright red, and she was trembling.

"Mommy, please. Mr. Joe's real nice. He's my friend. He never did anything to hurt me," sobbed Miranda.

"Darling, everything is all right. Mommy loves you. Let's go home and bake your special cake. Everything's okay now." said the mother. She turned to Old Joe and said curtly, "I regret my actions."

Then she held out a ten dollar bill, careful not to make physical contact, saying, "Will this suffice?"

"I 'spect so," said Joe.

Then she jerked Miranda away and walked rapidly toward their car.

Then Old Joe said softly, "Go wit God if he'll go wit you."

They did not hear him.

CATFISH JOE, THE DRUG DEALER

Old Joe won five hundred on the lottery and felt like the richest son of a bitch in west Philly. And he thought, "When you is high, roll. And when you is low, don' bitch. God don' want Ol' Joe to be stingy wit' hisself or nobody else. It aint no good when you is gone." In this vein he was dressed in a purple suit, black shirt, and red tie and he sported a rather large Zircon ring. "A man just aint a man widout' the Bling," he thought.

He was at the classiest strip club in West Philly, The Top Hat. None of the strippers were blind, crippled, or smelling Godawful rotten.

He rather fancied himself to be like Richard Roundtree out of Shaft, "a complicated man, no one understands him but his woman." The powerfual voice of B.B. King wafted through the air, "The thrill is gone. Gone for good, I'm free, free, free from your spell. And all I can do is wish you well." Over all, he was feeling like a man of the world, sophisticated and wise. "I sho' be gittin' me some tonight."

As if in answer to this prayer, Tamika, one of the bar girls. slithered over. Her stage name was "Sweet and Low" and she was both, generally speaking. "Mr. Joe, I heard you was flush tonight. Aint nobody ever take it with 'em. Besides they aint no fuckin' in the grave, sugar."

She squeezed his arm and a vision of her six inch chartreuse nails squeezing his dick gave him a hard on.

"Don' you worry, Gal. later on Ol' Joe sho' open yo' sweet flower and do what he do." And he noted her tiny breasts, like two thumb tacks on cardboard and her glorious ass. It was the kind of ass as seen in men's magazines, fat, high, rounded, and one could place two martinis on both cheeks and spill nary a drop. And as she undulated away, he thought, "That lil' Gal got true heart. Every damn bum what ast, she give him, one, maybe two dollars and she smile at him like he goddamned Cary Grant or somethin'. She be a God fearin' woman even if she make her livin' wid' her twat."

Then he saw them, two white boys, framed in bas relief at the door, as if they couldn't make up their minds whether they should come in or not. Old Joe chuckled and said, sotto voce, "Jellyfish. They looks like they be jellyfish and can't decide whether they should come in and get a beat down from the niggers in here." Then the boys singled out Joe for whatever reason and came over to his stool.

"Say, buddy," said the braver one, "We were wondering if you could sell us some White Lady?" The boy cocked his head to the side like an Eminem CD cover and looked down at his expensive Nike sneakers.

"You wants yoself' some heron (heroin), boy?" queried Joe.

"No, Sir," he replied, "We meant cocaine." He blushed cherry blossom pink. "Why aint you jes' say so. That be crack. White Lady be somethin' else entirely. You don' go ordering jes' any damn ol' thing. Might kill yo' damn ass! Now you tells me why you done pick Ol' Joe out of everyone in here. You don' think the young bloods in they hang down jeans, tee shirts, tattoos and Bling out they asses don' got no drugs?"

There was a shifting of feet and a nervous glancing around.

"Well, we thought you looked like the richest person in here," said Blondie, the brave one.

"That's right, sir," said the other one, a nondescript whelp of a boy. So nondescript as to make a blank sheet of paper seem fascinating.

"Well, you boys sure done hit the nail on the head. Ol' Joe be the meanest, baddest, most evil motherfucker that ever lived! Don mess wit Joe, he jes as soon cap ya as look at ya. Why ya' looks like an entire fantasy palace be dancin' in yo' head?"

"We just want to get high. Everyone's doing it," replied Blondie.

"If everyone gone stick a sharp pole up they asses, you gone do that too, boy?" asked Joe.

"Look," said Blondie, showing his impatience, "Are you going to sell us the coke or not?"

"Sho', said Old Joe. "You ever seen a bidness man who don' want to make a buck? I got to keep up my lavish life style." Then he took a mighty slug of his blackberry brandy and coughed fiercely.

"This fuckin' stuff gone kill me but I likes to choose the way in which I goes. Don't want no train to hit me or no cinder block to fall on my godamned head. 'Spose ya lets Ol' Catfish Joe buy ya a beer or a brandy or somethin'. After all, we's bidness partners."

"Mister, we just want to score. That's all," said Blondie.

"I jes' likes to be cordial. Ya know seal it wid' a kiss," said Mr. Joe.

Blondie jumped back like he'd heard a rattlesnake.

"No, boy you is too literal minded. Ol' Joe don' roll that way. Strictly T and A. No dick, whatsoever. What yo' names. boys?

"I don't see the relevance of this," said Blondie, "but I'm Tray and he's Bobby. We're from Chestnut Hill."

"A word of advice," said Old Joe. "Don' you never bring yo' white asses down here late at night again. They some boys here who cut the balls off white boys fo' just lookin' at 'em. And another thing I got to tell ya is yo' body is God's temple and you gone befoul it. Adam and Eve done got kicked out of the Garden of Eden fo' just this same kind of shit."

"What the fuck! Are you a preacher or a dealer?" asked Blondie.

"Relax, young blood. I gives this lecture to everyone. It be like the surgeon general's warning on a pack of cigarettes. "This shit gone kill ya, but go ahead if ya still wants to."

"You're weird, old man," said Tray.

"Yes, God done blessed me that way," said Mr. Joe.

"Old man, you're getting on my last nerve. I'm going to snap!" said Tray. His face was flushed like a broken valentine candy and it wouldn't have said, 'Be Mine'.

"Relax yoself', youngster. Life aint be all that tragic," said Joe. "I takes yo' money now and you takes this here address. Okay, son?"

After they left, Tyrone, Joe's de facto God son, came over to see where Joe had sent them.

Joe doubled over in laughter. "Tyrone, I done sent them to Madame Elsie's Ho House on Ogontz Avenue. Fuckin' be a damn site better fo' them than snortin' coke!"

"But they smells like bologna, Mr. Joe, and they aint wash they things!" said Tyrone.

"Aint a man alive who don' like bologna," said Mr. Joe.

They both had a real laugh riot. A real long one.

Two hours later, two wild eyed white boys made their second entrance. They had the look of two very pissed game cocks. Ferocious but too small. Way too small.

"And just where is my goddamned money, old man? You sent us to a fucking whore house!" screamed Tray.

Several young bloods moved closer surrounding the boys. The bar glasses sparkled like smudgy diamonds and the cigarette smoke made blue paisley patterns in the air and Percy Sledge's "When a Man Loves a Woman" blasted from the jukebox.

"Mr. Joe, they hasslin' you? Want us to straighten out they asses," said one strapping young blood.

"No, Ol' Joe got this one, boys. It seems as if you is a tad upset wid' Ol' Joe. Does I perceive the sicheeashun kerreckly?"

"Damned straight! You sent us to a whore house!" screamed Tray.

"I thought that was what you really wanted and was too shy to ask," said Joe, incredulously.

"Not what we wanted!" said Blondie.

"I'm shocked. All white boys wants black pussy. It be real juicy and the bitch can go all night long...if you got the right equipment, that is. Black men got it goin' on that fo' sho'"

"And what about AIDS and other STD'S," said Blondie.

"Boy, you crazy in yo' natural mind. Everybody know they pussys be made of tin. Aint nobody ever get no aids and shit from no black ho! You seen the big gal wit' the orange hair and bright blue lightening bolt goin' down the middle of her head? That be Ol' Joe's Precious Darlin'. She charge twenty dollars for a throw down on her back. She charge Ol' Joe one hundred dollars 'cause I be a tad freaky. Nothin' real bad though. I aint be layin' no hurt on no po', sweet woman. That be jes' evil. And I be one wit' the Lord. He walks wit' me, and he talks wit' me And he tells me I am his Own."

"Can we just get our damn money back,"said Blondie."Sho, you can, Blondie, or rather, Tray," replied Mr. Joe. "But Ol' Joe really got some fine blow fo' you. It make you think yo' ass in Arkansas, yo' head in the Himalayas, and Charlie Byrd be doin' a riff just fo' you, and you be ballin' some real pretty, blond, angel ass. Stick wid' Ol' Joe. I aint steer you wrong."

The boys hesitated, looked at one another, and tried to read minds. It was a failed attempt. Empty air cannot transcend itself.

"Well, where is it? You got it on you?" asked Tray.

"Does I look like I carries contraband on me, boy? Drug dealers is sneaky bastards or aint you know that? I spec' I takes you to my crib so's we can do bidness. You boys is from good homes, is you?" asked Mr. Joe.

My dad's a criminal lawyer," said Tray.

"My mom's a CEO for the phone company," said Pale Boy.

"Do that 'C' stand for cunt, boy?" laughed Mr. Joe.

"It stands for Company Executive Officer, and I'll thank you not to cast aspersions on my mom's character!" said Pale Boy.

"I 'spec it be true on some level, She got you in her belly, aint she? Women is all Bitches, It be God's Master Plan."

"How'd you like it if I popped you one old man?" said the Pale One.

Joe gestured to the open room, and said, "I 'spec you don' want to do that, son."

"Let's get on with it. We're in a hurry." snapped Tray.

"You 'bout to have one of the greatest experiences of yo' life, Tray. Aint no hurry up. Ol' Joe like to interview his clients. I can afford to be choosy. Tell me 'bout yoselves."

"I don't see how this is relevant," said Tray.

"It be relevant to me, Ol' Catfish Joe. You don' worry 'bout it. It be my bidness."

"All right, I'll play along, you crazy old coot," said Tray. "Bobby and I live in Chestnut Hill. I have two sisters and we're the Brady Bunch. Bobby lives alone with his mom.

"Does you like pussy?" asked Mr. Joe, and Tray nodded.

"I can see you is off to a bang up start. But. yo' friend, Bobby. Be a little limp wrested and a tad swishy. I be kind of concerned fo' him."

"Oh, for crying out loud. Everyone thinks I'm gay. I am really, really, really tired of this shit. What am I supposed to do, put on a chain around my chest and bust it like Hercules?"said Bobby.

"Wouldn't be such a bad idea," said Mr. Joe with a gentle smile. "Would you say you was rich?" asked Joe.

"Comparatively," replied Tray.

"Compared to all the other unlucky sons of bitches in this world," said Mr. Joe with a guffaw.

"You got both parents, aint you, Tray, and they aint got a rat's ass where you is now, right?" asked Joe. "And you aint got a man in yo' life right now, Bobby?"

"No, mom divorced him when I was five. She said he was a real mean bastard."

"Bobby, I may not be 'xactly what you had in mind but I sho' be glad to takes ya out fo' a burger or to go bowlin' sometime. I thinks ya needs to know some shit and it be important," said Joe. After all, I aint a dealer all the time just some of the time.

Bobby, somewhat taken aback, said softly, "Why thank you Mr. Joe."

"I can't help but think this is not the way a regular dealer acts," said Tray.

"I aint done nothin' regular my whole life 'cept shittin'" said Mr. Joe. "Back to you, Tray is you happy wit yo' life?"

"My parents are idiots. All they ever think about is money. And when I go to them with my problems, they just throw money at me," replied Tray.

"Does you have enough to eat and a good place to sleep?" asked Joe.

"Well, doesn't everyone?" queried Tray.

"Son, that be too stupid a question to even answer," said Joe.

"Well, it's only because they're not educated," replied Tray.

"You one of the great thinkers of our time, Tray. 'Spose we just burn them in Hell, too," exclaimed Mr. Joe.

"My parents don't love me. All they care about is their damn status symbols!"

"I sees ya gots one of them fancy Izod tee shirts on. If you is so plain how come you aint in burlap or some shit," queried Joe.

"I gone tell a story 'bout love. I was born into a sharecropper family in Arkansas and they was thirteen of us chillen. In the summer, the heat fry us and in winter, we done froze. We et one meal a day and daddy he always owe the company sto'. We et ham, grits, eggs, and cornbread, and sometimes, they wasn't nothin'. My daddy, he done beat us fierce and mostly fo' no reason at all. And he don' spare the rod. Moms be too busy wid the babies hanging off her tits to defend us none. I growed much larger than pops but I never whupped him even though I could

I knew he love us when I seed his red hands from pickin' the cotton, and when I see my meals at night. His love be silent. The Lord's love also be silent but it always be wid you. Tray, anybody who tell ya they loves ya all the time, be messin' wid ya. They wants somethin'. True love be silent and cool like the wind, and furthermo' why ya wants to go off and fry yo' brain, the masterpiece God done gave you out of the goodness and mercy of his heart?" queried Mr. Joe.

"Are you a preacher or a dealer, Mr. Joe?"

"I be a God fearin' dealer. I only sells to Bad Asses. Fuckers that got taranchulas in they hearts who cap they own grannies in they beds fo' a fix!"

"You mean you were never going to sell to us?" asked Tray.

"They may be some truth in that," said Joe with a slight smile.

"Mr. Joe, you're not even a real dealer, are you?" asked Bobby.

"Also, some truth there," said Mr. Joe with a big wide grin.

"I got this to say to you, young bloods. If you goes and fucks wid' the drug scene, you in fo' a world of hurt. Suffering don't teach a body anything 'cept they wants it to stop. Those what recommends it, recommends it fo' others, not theyselves! Another thing, I best not see yo' silly young asses in here again cuz if one of the bloods don' git ya, Ol' Joe gone do you hisself."

"Part time hit man," said Tray.

"You amazingly smart, boy," said Mr. Joe.

MIZ LUCILLE

Every time Lucille passed a man on the street, he would hear snatches of the song, "Lucille, please come back where you belong. Lucille..." She was white, a ferociously striking beauty, but inside, she was as gentle as the "Lamb of God." She was six feet tall, a natural platinum haired blond, and fifty years old. When her husband's pension ran out she went back to work as a pole dancer in an exclusive black men's strip club. She was the star attraction. There was nary a wrinkle on her lovely, Skandanavian face. Her brutally, beautiful, pouting lips made a man think of all the nasty things he could do with them. She was a confectioner's angel whom everyone wanted to tarnish. Pull the angel from the heavens and roll in the mud with her like a nasty beast with no act denied.

Lucille had the look of a high fashion model, thin, leggy, and angular. She never just walked, she sauntered down the street. She cut arcs in the pale summer air with her razor sharp hip bones. Her blue eyes had the cast of the night sky before it drops into darkness, a strange kind of indigo or violet blue. A man could close his eyes and still see her magnificent orbs, remembering them as if they had been burned into his brain.

This particular day, Old Joe was on his way to a modern literature class at Penn in university city. He audited the courses of his liking and gave many a classroom a lively discussion or debate. He thought of his mind as tract of land. "You done give it to me, Lord. And now, it up to me to plant somethin' on it! Aint nobody like no blank slate." Later on, he learned the white term for this was, "tabula rosa." Then he saw the ugly scenario enfolding before his eyes. Two angry, black, welfare mothers were terrorizing Miz Lucille.

"Go back to where yo' 'blongs, white 'ho. Ya don' 'blong here wid' yo' ol' nasty white twat," screamed one, who gave Lucille a shove. Joe could see her lurching bulk and thought to himself, "She done had too many goddamned Big Macs and fries!"

The other "young lady", if one could call her such, was even more vicious. She had three young toddlers in tow, and one in the 'oven."

'What is yo' doin' wid' our mens, ya slut? Ya best stay away from black dick if ya knows what is good fo' ya! Ya sticks to yo' own kind, heah me, bitch? Whatsa matter, can't find they lil' gnat dicks, do that be it?"

Lucille said nothing but quickened her pace. Mr. Joe knew she was terrified and trying not to show it. He knew her heart was beating frantically like a small bird caught in an iron cage.

He stepped in. "Girls, jes' why is yo' fuckin' wid' Miz Lucille? She aint done nothin' to ya. What ya got to say, Rashida?"

"She stank, Mr. Joe," replied Rashida. "She old enough to be a grandmother and still shakin' her booty. And she git money fo' her ass. It jes' aint right. It be a sin."

"And when the Lord appoint you his watch dog? Recall the scripture, "Judge Not Lest Ye Be Judged?" How this not apply to you? And besides, ya done had three kids out of wedlock. Ya thinks the Lord condone that?"

"Mr. Joe, you know that aint the same. What I done I done fo' love. I aint no ho!" said Rashida.

"And look at yersef, youngster. Who you think gone pay fo' yo' fat dinosaur ass? Ya probly' has to pay the mens to be wit you!" exclaimed Mr. Joe.

Rashida, tearing up, said, "Mr. Joe, why you even go there?"

"And what about you, Kadisha? Ya done put up three chillens fo' adoption. When the Lord say, "Go Forth And Multiply," ya think he be talking directly to you? Or is you the Old Woman in the Shoe?"

"That aint even the same, Mr. Joe. I aint never take no money fo' my ass. And why is you so damn mean?"

"Oh, like you aint take a fifty here and there fo' some pampers, or formula or shit?" queried Mr. Joe.

"That aint even the same, Mr. Joe. He do it cuz he love me," replied Kadisha.

"And is he wid' ya now, Gal," queried Mr. Joe. "Youngster, it all a matter of degree, but it be the same. Only she be mo' honest and ask fo' it up front and she git a damn site mo' fo' it than you! And Kadisha, ya falls in love a helluva lot. Why aint ya git some job trainin' and guit bein' a five dollar ho'?" said Mr. Joe.

"Go Fuck yersef," screamed Kadisha.

"Would if I could," replied Mr. Joe. "It do seem like a good idea. Now, I 'spec you youngsters better get yo' fat Macdonalds eatin' asses on out of here cuz' what you is doin' is called assault, and I've a mind to call the po-lice. I be testifying agin' ya in court! Damned straight!"

The girls disbanded immediately and made themselves scarce. It was if they were jackals knocked off the food wagon by larger prey. Lucille stood glimmering in the sun like a day time angel, and Joe thought to himself, "I aint never seen no one shine like this befo'". He noticed the diamond chandelier ear rings and the choker she wore and surmised they were real. Whatever Miz Lucille wore was of quality, even her stripper costume. She went under the name of "Scarlet, the Harlot."

" So, is you okay now, Miz Lucille?" asked Joe.

"I'm fine, Mr. Joe, and I'd like to repay your kindness."

Joe decided to remain silent, He wasn't no damn hound dog to take advantage of a lady. He was with the Lord.

"Come over this Sunday for High Tea!" intoned Miz Lucille.

"What you mean by high, Miz Lucille? Ol' Joe don't do no powders or shit."

Lucille laughed and it was like tiny bells breaking into pieces.

"Don't worry, Mr. Joe, I've got nothing stronger than brandy or champagne," she replied.

At three sharp, he rang her door bell. He was dressed in his best brown suit from K Mart, and had a white kerchief in his lapel and his old shoes were polished as well as they could be. She opened the door and he handed her a bouquet of yellow and red tulips, and her entire face lit up in a kind of silver, white luminescence. "She make her livin' as a 'ho but she shine like a damn angel," he thought.

She had on a long, silver and pink, floral kimono and her platinum hair was like a silver river flowing down her back. The scent of dead roses in a closed room assailed his nostrils. It was a haunting scent, her scent.

The color scheme of her mansion could best be described as gentle, with pastel oranges, pinks and greens. The affect was one of abundance and comfort.

She poured tea water from a silver pot, and Mr. Joe thought, "Dang, if this aint be something Cary Grant be doin' in some old movie!" It was a world removed from Tastee Cakes and Hostess HoHo's. He liked the harsh, bitter chocolate mousse cake and the tart, fluffy lemon cake. She explained to him how lemon zest makes the lemon flavor stronger.

She told him that the mansion was purchased by her late husband, a railroad baron. He had rescued her from The Life. She explained that she used to strap a small hunting knife between her legs and said, "It's good to be brave and better to be careful." As she mentioned this to Mr. Joe, visions of the streets flooded her mind like an evil Fassbinder movie. All movement was odious and distasteful, and the smell was rank like that of a dead deer. Entire scenes came back flooded with a magenta light. She shuddered and Mr. Joe knew to change the direction of the conversation.

She talked of her dead husband with extreme fondness and her sorrow at never being able to have children. Mr. Joe knew she was grateful to him but did not love him and he also knew she was eternally faithful while he lived. But she never actually said these things: Mr. Joe's specialty was reading between the lines. "She done live her life like a cut rose in a vase," he thought.

She never tried to be an actress or a model. She never tried to be anything other than what she was. Beauty was her poetry to the world.

Her only poetry. Under her gentleness, buried real deep, was a tigress, and this was why men kept coming back to see her dance. To possess her somehow. Miz Lucille also asked Joe about himself and when she found out or surmised how roughly he was living she offered him a part time job as estate manager and a small room off the back of her house.

"I 'spec I takes the job, Miz Lucille. I be gittin' a iil' tired of them catfish. Sometimes, they got three eyes and shit, and I gits this creepy feelin' they is starin' at me as I eats them," replied Mr. Joe.

"Oh, we can do a lot better than catfish, Mr. Joe. I am a Cordon Bleu chef. I do all my own cooking. You can eat until you burst!"

Then she let one of her high, elegant breasts slip out of her kimono, and just smiled softly at Mr. Joe. Mr. Joe's eyes got real warm and soft and he gently placed one hand on her forearm.

"Miz Lucille, you don' want ol' Joe. I be a ramblin' man and besides I got me a main bitch, name of Etta. She find I mess wid' a white woman, she gone come here and cut off both of yo' tits. Ya needs a real man to spear ya through the heart and sear yo' loins wid' the fire of hell. I holds ya special in my heart, Miz Lucille, like somethin' fine and pure."

"Mr. Joe, I'm just a whore."

"No, no you aint, Miz Lucille. Ever hear of Mary Magdalene? She be Jesus's main disciple, and she be a whore. You got a powerful goodness inside ya, and I sees it clear enough. Does I still got the job or is you mad wit Ol' Joe?"

"Yes," replied Lucille, "Of course you have the job."

"Miz Lucille, I kind of loved ya from afar fo' some time now and I be carryin' a poem in my pocket fo' ya waitin fo' jes' the right time to give it to ya. Now be that time. I gives it to ya but don' open 'til I be gone, okay?" said Mr. Joe. "It be called 'My Soft, Sweet Pearl'."

She waited until he had left and then opened it. And the pure, simple power of the words pierced her gentle, fine heart and she raised up her arms in the still air of the room as if to embrace the face of God.

NEVERMO'

Old Joe was on his way home from Etta's and the moon was like a newly minted silver quarter that followed him as he shuffled down the raw umber road. Joe thought," Aint it curious how things keeps they colors even in total darkness!" Then he thought, "Joe, you done think some dumb ass things when it coulda' been somethin' that really tilt the world on its ass!"

Some people thought computers, guns, or stocks controlled the world. Old Joe believed that thoughts controlled the world and that they issued directly from God. Or The Other Fellow. He and Etta had a mutual agreement. When he needed her, he came. When he needed solitude, he left, and vice versa. Ty was like a human telegraph between them and didn't seem to mind.

As Old Joe approached the entrance to his shack at the gray slat entrance he saw a flurry of wings and heard an ungodly sound like that of a "shade". In black vernacular this translates as "spirit."

He stopped and saw an evil, glaring pair of tiny red eyes and he thought,

"Dang, let me git' the shot gun and blast the sucka'" He heard a second flurry of wings and saw the silhouette of a flying raven in the moonlight. He heard its cry and thought, "like a sound from Hell.' It might have said a word. He didn't catch it and shuddered. "Dang," he thought, "a grown man afraid of a damn bird. What he gon' do peck me on my head! Then the next day he went to do his chores at Miz Lucille's, cutting the lawn, planting bulbs, cleaning the porches, and organizing her disastrous garage.

He drank multiple glasses of her tart lemonade and ate the two gigantic ham and cheese sandwiches she left for him. He noted the nutty brown bread she used and thought to himself, "White people! They always gots to be diffrent'!"

He decided not to stay at his cozy room at Lucille's and to go back to his lone shack. He was in no mood for woman folk, black or white. His thoughts started to wander, "A man just like a wolf sometimes. He like to be by hisself." The vast black velvet sky thrilled him and he felt his man's heart slip out through his mouth like a vapor. The moon was a sly, glistening sliver in the night sky. Things lurched and slithered in their own night symphony and he was glad he could not see them. "Don' want to see the Devil neither," he mused. "Fat ladies' asses alone be enough to discombobulate Ol' Joe!"

When he got to the cabin he saw the hated bird had returned. "It's eyes look 'zaxtly like two pieces of coal from Hell! That bastard give me the creeps like he a 'shade'. Then these words fled from Old Joe's mouth,

"Once 'pon a midnight dreary, while I pondered weak and weary,
Over many a quaint and curious volume of ancient lore,
While I nods, nearly nappin' suddenly there be a tappin'
As if someone be gently rappin', rappin' at my goddamn do'.
It be some visitor, I mutters, tappin' at my goddamn do'
Only this and nothin' mo"

The Old Joe went out and found only a single raven feather.

"He lettin' me know I aint never gone' catch 'em. It seem he got a hard on for' me and I loves animals. 'Specially steak."

The next morning when Joe went to the creek to get water, the bird was nowhere to be found. "Maybe he evil but he sho' he aint no natural fool neither. He know I be shootin' his ass if I sees him."

So Joe went off to town to get staples like potatoes, beans, rice, carrots, apples, and coffee. Only he called them victuals. People often remarked that Joe cooked by fire and had no stove. But Joe would replay, "Aint no 'thang. What about people wid' cancer or aids? Now that truly be a bitch. People done bitch too damn much anyhow. They credit cards gits' too dang high and they practically has a heart attack!

And they done it to theyselves. Screw yosef' aint 'jes no phrase! It be a solid practice!" Ol' Joe don' live high on the hog but he git' what he need. People done say a po' ass man can't git' no pussy. That be a total fuckin' lie. Depends on yo' natural charm and such. I aint 'splain what such mean. No need."

He hung around town with the old men at the barber shop and each spread his old, fond memories out like a strand of pearls. Joe knew he had the gift of books which they did not yet said nothing. They saw no need for any book reading outside of the Scriptures. He thought fondly of Shakespeare's Hamlet. "When life break yo' heart, it git' interestin'. Hamlet be my boy," mused Joe.

In the back of his mind, Joe was thinking, "I know I be hangin' back cuz' I dreads goin' home. They be somethin' supernatural 'bout that fuckin' raven. Why he want to mess wid' me so much? I done everythin' I could to let 'em know he aint welcome."

He paused and further contemplated his dilemma. "Somethin' bitchy 'bout that raven like he aint a he but a she. And I gits a weird thought in my head like this be the spirit of my late wife, Lenore. I gone tell ya 'bout Lenore. When we was together, she done want me to go down on her every night. Almost got lock jaw! It stank powerful bad like the pit of Hell or a giant pile of dead cats even wid' the drug sto' shit or vinegar. Sometimes, I spent the night in the fields and never tol' her the problem. She think it be another bitch and get to hittin' me wid the cast iron skillet. My head still ring sometime or I think it do. She was a good woman though, did the cookin', the cleanin', fed the dog, and me. We never had no kids or shit. Then we finds out she got the cancer down below, and six months later she gone.

Befo' she go she pull me close and say wid' her dry scaly lips, "Darlin',

promise me whether we're in heaven or in hell, we'll always be together." I promised but to be honest, I was a tad relieved. They lots in the of flowers in the field, all smellin' different'. And now I think she know I aint keep the promise!

"Prophet! Says I, thing of evil, prophet still if you is bird or devil,

By that heaven that bends above us, by all that God we both adore,

Tell this soul with sorrow laden, it shall clasp a sainted maiden
Whom the angels named Lenore.
Clasp a rare and radiant maiden whom the angels call Lenore.
Quoth the Raven, "Nevermo'."

"Oh shit," said Joe. 'She in the wrong place! Dang, aint that a bitch! She still kickin' my ass even when she dead. The bird departed and never came back.

STRAIGHT FROM THE HORSE'S ASS

"Ty," said Old Joe, " I done tol' yo' Grams I gone straighten out yo' young ass. It come straight from the horse's ass like a pile of hot shit. It be the only place strong enough fo' yo' dumb self. Life aint no magical thing son. 'Ya think it glisten, 'ya think it flash like teeth at midnight, or sparkle like a damned diamond on a fat bitch's neck? It aint nothin' but time and a half and a 401K. Dollars is mo' powerful than blood, son. 'Ya got yo' body, Ty. God done give it to you. But you aint got no money, son. God aint gone give you that. 'Ya got to fuck 'wid the devil every day of yo' natural life to git' that. 'Ya got to serve someone. 'Git me, motherfucker?

'Oh, shit, Mr. Joe. Whatcha gone say? That I go'in to Hell or to jail, and I gone be some fucked up "whitie's"bitch? Mr. Joe I aint never git' caught. I runs too fast. I were a track star."

"And you thinks the po-lice aint got no track stars, or what if they jes' caps ya? Ya thinks 'whitie" don' enjoy cappin' some black ass?" asked Mr. Joe. "Yo' head aint jes' be some decoration on top of yo' head. It be fo' cogitation! Yo' head is a tabula rosa!"

"A what, Mr. Joe? Where yo git' all them white words?" asked TY

"It mean blank slate, youngster. You is a whole lot of nothin' and you aint never gone have nothin'!"

"You aint got nothin' yerself, Mr. Joe," replied Ty.

"Ideas, boy. I gots ideas, and ideas cuts deeper than a sword."

"Now, you is jes' talkin' shit, Mr. Joe," replied Ty.

"I knew you wasn't no deep thinker, Ty. Now I tries a diffrent' approach. What yo'math and and science grades, boy?"

"A's and B's, Mr. Joe," he replied.

"That be the nail that stick, Ty. You done git yo' diploma?" asked Joe.

"Sho', Grams say she fill my ass wid' buckshot if I don't."

"A wonderful strategy, boy," said Joe.

"I aint like it none. It were hard," replied the boy.

"Dang, boy, is you some kind of goddamned idiot? That why they calls it "work". It aint 'sposed to be easy. Ol' Joe be a boxer in his twenties to age thirty-five gittin' his royal ass kicked and kickin' ass hisself. Does you think it were easy?"

"Well, I aint like that kind of thing, Mr. Joe. Too violent, and might git' yo' head scrambled some kind of way," replied Ty.

"Oh, now you is objectin' to violence, Ty. What 'bout when ya jacks off them ol' ladies fo' they social security checks?"

"It aint nothin' unless they falls down or some shit. I tries to be kind," replied Ty.

"Ty, you is all heart, a real humanitarian," replied old Joe.

"Where is you gittin' all them white words, Mr. Joe," asked Ty.

"I goes to Penn, Ty, and audits they courses," replied Joe.

"What fo"? You aint git' nothin' fo' it, Mr. Joe," replied Ty.

"I holds the whole fuckin' world in my head, Ty. It worth mo' than the Bling, mansions and cars. Any goddamned thing."

"You talkin' crazy, Mr. Joe. One too many to yo' head," replied Ty.

"I tries another path wid' you, youngster," replied Mr. Joe. "Ty, you aint never been to Chestnut Hill, Bryn Mawr, or Paoli?"

"Sho', and yo' point, Mr. Joe?" replied Ty.

"You see what 'whitie" got? Ya know how he got all them things, Ty?"

"It be in the fambly'. They passes it down," replied Ty, somewhat sheepishly.

"That aint even it, dumb ass! Billie Holliday say, "God Bless the Child That Has His Own". "Whitie" study and he work fo' it! It don't come easy. Ya thinks studyin' stop when ya gits out of high school. It don' never stop if you is bright, if ya knows the truth in this world. Ya thinks truth be many things. Diffrent' fo' each person. Truth be only one thing fo' everyone. God make it that way!" intoned Mr.

Joe. "I know you aint no deep thinker as I already done said. But ya understands math, boy. The mo' ya learns, the mo' ya earns. I gone take ya' to see Mamie Dukes now, Ty."

"What fo', Mr. Joe. She stink to high heaven and besides, I done mugged her once," replied Ty.

"She aint gon' see ya, Ty, or anythin' else ever agin' in this world. She dead, Ty. Kilt by an addict last night in her own bed."

"I don' want to see that shit, Mr. Joe. I aint no killer," replied Ty.

"People don' start out as killers and pieces of shit, Ty. They starts out jes' like you, kinda' bad but no big deal. Then they changes. They evolves, Ty," said Mr. Joe.

"I aint do it, Mr. Joe. I refuses. Ya hear, Mr. Joe?" asked Ty.

"You aint never in yo' life refuse Ol' Joe. I can break ya, boy, like a fuckin' match stick and I damn sure will." He roughly grabbed Ty's arm and guided him forcibly down the street. The boy was afraid and went along. When they got there, the policemen were grouped about. Joe took one aside and talked briefly to him. Ty could not hear their conversation. Old Joe came over and said brusquely, "Boy, we go'in in and I aint takin' no shit from you!"

"See, Ty, all she ever done was give to other people and she aint never had no real money herself. Whoever come, she feed him, and give him money to stay out of the fuckin' cold. This world be a mean, bad ass place and she jes' want to make it a better place. She were a smart woman, Ty, and probly' saw the bastard fo' what he were but she think she can bathe him in God's love."

Ty looked over and tried to keep the vomit from rising. The smell of death and putrefaction was overwhelming and flies swarmed around her purple twisted lips. Her dress was pulled up obscenely to her waist showing her old, yellowed slip and underwear as if some sexual congress had taken place. She was eighty-two and the gray roots in her red orange hair showed up brutally in the harsh overhead light. Ty ran wildly from the room and wretched violently in the yard. Nothing came up. A policeman came over and put a sympathetic hand on his shoulder.

Mr. Joe came out, pulled Ty up, and straightened his collar. Ty looked into Old Joe's eyes and saw a coloration he had never seen before. He saw worlds in those eyes, and a paralyzing pain, and an obdurate, absolute power.

"Boy, we gon' make some changes, now. You gon' go upstate to a junior college to briing yoself' up to speed. You gon' be as good as "whitie",even better. Then dependin' how ya does, you gon' go to Penn or Temple on a work study scholarship. They aint gon' be no rippin' and tearin', do'in shots in Mexico, and slippin' yo' dick in white girls. Ya hear?" asked Mr. Joe

"I aint do any of that shit, Mr. Joe," replied Ty.

"You aint shit, boy, but you will be," replied Old Joe. I be you don' know ol' Tennesee Ernie Ford's song, "Sixteen Tons."

It go:

"Sixteen tons, what do you get,

Another day older and deeper in debt.

My right fist's of iron,

My left one's of steel.

If the right one don't get you,

The left one will."

Then Mr. Joe hauled off and decked Ty completely knocking him on his ass.

Ty got up slowly, red faced, and almost in tears, and said, "Officer! Officer! He done assault me! You seed it!"

"You boys seen anything," asked Joe in a casual way.

"Nope. Not a damn thing," replied one. The others just looked like bored versions of television cops.

"Grams gone fuck ya over fo' this, Mr. Joe! She gone press charges!" stuttered the boy.

"Oh, I don' know if ya wants to do that, youngster. Me, and Etta got that one covered, too," said Joe in a lackadaisical fashion.

"What the fuck is you talkin' 'bout, Mr. Joe?" asked Ty.

"Ever think the term, motherfucker, be not just a phrase, but a practice? Ya gits in a whole mess of trouble if ya actually does it. Like jail or the head shop," explained Mr. Joe.

"So what this got to do wid' me?" asked the boy.

"Son, yo' Grams, Etta, don' play. She figure if you gon' be a fuckup anyway why not jes' throw yo' ass in jail sooner rather than later. They got places fo' boys wid' unnatural desires fo' they female relatives."

"But I aint done none of that shit. Never would. That be just plain perverted!" said Ty, really appalled.

"But if she say you do it, Ty," said Joe, pausing for effect.

"She never fuck me over like that, Mr. Joe!" exclaimed Ty.

Mr. Joe allowed himself to have a laugh riot. A really Big one.

"Son, you aint really know yo' Grams, Etta. If a man fuck her over she aint got no qualms whatsoever 'bout running a butcher knife right under his damn ribs. Do that sound plausible to you, Ty?" asked Joe

Ty nodded silently and said not a word. He took on the aspect of a worn shirt that's been washed one time too many.

"It be a beautiful day, Ty. Jes' beautiful," said Mr. Joe smiling real big like the state of Texas.

MR. JOE AND THE GAYS

"What is you sayin', boy? Is you fuckin' wid' Ol' Joe?"

"No, sir, we'll pay you one thousand dollars a day for a fashion shoot. We want our models shot with real people, construction workers, pizza parlor workers, men in barber shops, and the like. You know, the working man."

"Why you aint jes' say ugly old black fuckers like yerself?" asked Mr. Joe.

"Granted," replied the Boy of Swish. "I just didn't want to offend you."

"How you figure the truth offend Ol' Joe? Ol' Joe be wid' the Lord and the Lord command him to tell the truth."

"We want people with character faces," said the Boy of Swish. Joe noted his skin was as soft and rosy as a Peace Rose. He wore a hot pink Izod Lacoste tee shirt and khaki Ralph Lauren pants with no socks for his expensive penny loafers.

"Well I aint be crazy in the head so I says yes. One thousand dollars buys a whole lot of beans and shit," replied Joe.

The boy handed him an expensive, one hundred dollar pen in which to sign the contract. And Joe thought, "Them smooth hands aint never seen a hammer or a nail. He been signin' greetin' cards and jerkin' off dick."

"I'm Kevin, the stylist. I get you ready for the shoot," his voice was crisp and high.

"By ready, what does you mean?" queried Joe.

"Don't worry straight is definitely not my type! I mean the clothes, the make-up, the way the clothes hang. I get the models ready for the photographer."

"Fo' a thousand dollars a day, ya can make me up as Mae West! What the fuck I care?" replied Old Joe.

"I doubt it will come to that," said Kevin hiding a smile with his hand. He was starting to like the "old fucker". "We're going to put you with beautiful models at various working sites through out the city."

"Oh, that jes' be a capital idea. Ol' Joe wid' a skinny gal on one arm, a hammer in another, and a giant hard-on."

"That would only add to the ambiance," replied Kevin.

"I know what ambiance mean, Kevin, and I thinks ya is serious. Ya aint worry 'bout size in black men?" asked Mr. Joe.

"Never did before," replied Kevin with a broad laugh.

"Now I know you is my man, Kevin," said Mr. Joe.

"But, not in that way," quipped Kevin.

"When I gone start?" asked Joe.

"Today," replied Kevin, handing him a rough plaid shirt, worker's jeans, and Timberline boots with thick socks. "We have the tools on site, already," said Kevin.

"Can I keep the boots? They is expensive," asked Joe.

"Keep any thing but those stupid, skinny bitches. They're not any brighter than a twenty-five watt bulb. No wonder I like men!"

"I likes'em okay. But they can't do nothin' but sit on my face. Any other way, they gone break like fine crystal into a million pieces. Our woman got ass fo' miles and great big tits that slap upside yo' damn head!" exclaimed Mr. Joe. "And they smells like pussy not no fancy chemicals."

"A bit more information than I need, Joe," replied Kevin.

"I 'spect so. You aint assailed me 'bout yo' adventures on the high sea, Kevin," said Joe.

"Mr. Joe I'm going to take you to a club after we finish the shoots. Let me be your first gay friend!"

"Sho', Kevin, I really likes ya. I don' care if ya fucks snakes," said Joe.

"Only on Sunday, Mr. Joe," replied Kevin.

In the following days, Mr. Joe dragged ass all over New York. He was so many different kinds of workers, it was practically schizophrenic. Every time he was posed inaccurately for a given job, he kept his mouth shut whispering to himself, "one thousand dollars".

The models were puppets fashioned by Giapetto's magic knife come to life. They were sweet like sugar cane, graceful as deer, and fine ornaments for virtually any business titan's arm. But it all was as dust, destined to fade away. Real woman were solid, loving, vicious, and hungry for life, gluttonous even. They were blazingly vivid like cut arteries. Where there was intense love; there was lurking danger. Mr. Joe took the models, allowing them to be draped over him like so many pieces of colored confetti. They came in all colors, blonds, brunettes, redheads, and more rarely, those with raven colored hair. All were long legged and tall and coltish, and so thin as to give the impression of concentration camp victims. "They sho' got pretty skin," and this pleased him deeply. He did like beauty even though he knew he would never possess it. He also knew they were as flowers destined to fade.

In the final pictures and poster boards, it was Joe's face everyone noticed. Kevin told him he was a "star" and all of New York was interested in him. Several large magazines interviewed him and got lively copy. It was then that Kevin approached him with the "deal". He offered to be Joe's manager and take a certain percentage and handle all the PR, advertising and such. He also mentioned that being gay was not his life's work; that he was a Wharton graduate. Mr. Joe had heard of that "tear you a new one" school and he consented.

Mr. Joe then explained that he knew Wharton because he audited classes at Penn. He then proceeded to tell Kevin of some of the jobs he had after he quit boxing.

"I had me a real shitty job at this lunch counter. One day, I be moppin' and polishin' and generally bustin' my ass, and the owner tell me to stop and git' on over there and clean the counters. I tells him, 'Look, you aint see I be busy. I gits to it later when I be done.' He done call me a bunch of names, and I calls him some back. And he fire my ass and say I never work in that town ever agin'"

"Then I gits a job wit' the Post Office and I thinks I got it made, benefits, 401K, whatever the hell that be. I work in the sortin' department. I work as hard as I can and I be powerful strong. And the other workers bitch, and say I was workin' too fast, and make them look bad. Next thing I know, the big boys call me in and I say to them that I be do'in my dead level best and they say that be the problem. I be bad for morale and they can't have that. Nosiree!"

This hurt me so bad I stays drunk fo' two whole weeks. May have fucked cows, or sheep, or even, a queer. Excuse me, Kevin, a gay."

"Mr. Joe if you fucked one of us, he'd still be limping, and walkng bow legged!" laughed Kevin. "Think you can keep doing this kind of work, Mr. Joe?"

"Sho', Kevin. It be like transferin' out of hell into heaven. Easy as eatin' a vanilla ice cream cone!" replied Old Joe. "And Kevin, I been thinkin' 'bout the Lord and gays. They be such horrible shit go'in on in the world, I think he gon' let the gays slide! After all, you aint hurtin' nobody."

"For the most part,"Kevin replied archly. "I'm going to take you to your first gay club, Joe."

"I aint got no problem wid' that, Kevin. They aint pull down my pants or some shit,"said Joe.

"Not unless you want them to," said

"Sodom and Gomorah!" said Mr. Joe.

"You can stay on the lower floors, Mr. Joe and besides they'll know you're straight. Don't go on the upper floors, a lot goes on up there."

"I think ya may need the Lord, after all, Kevin," said Joe.

"We get our heaven right here on earth, "replied Kevin. "And Mr. Joe, do you fuck only female statues in church?"

"You is smarter than ya looks, Kevin, and ya got quite a bite to ya!" replied Old Joe.

"That's a given, Mr. Joe," replied Kevin.

The club was called The Steppes, and it was in central Philadelphia. There appeared to be two kinds of clientele, the prosperous, and the hustlers. Usually the prosperous in their designer ensembles and expensive understated jewelry got in with no hesitation on the part of the door man. Mr. Joe did not know he was looking at Oscar de La Renta, Calvin Klein, Ralph Lauren and others. They walked in coolness and self assurance, their wealth sealing off from the brutality of the world.

He saw the hustlers, their darting eyes, and cracked lips. There was a dull hardness to them like the look in the eyes of a kitten that has just dyed. "Fresh meat, only somewhat spoiled."

" Mr. Joe, we make the world a more beautiful place. More magic! It's the power of beauty, Mr. Joe. Why must life be so harsh?"

Then they went in, and Mr. Joe thought, "Boy, is you an ugly fucker compared to these mens!"

The inside was a cool green palace of black and green marble with two Art Nouveau Venus's on opposite sides of a large, dramatic dance floor. The floor was crowded with bare, sculpted, glistening chests and the song that was playing was "It's Raining Men." Old Joe thought God done give me a sign that he have a sense of irony.

Then Old Joe went to the antique wooden bar with the carved lilies and sat back in the plush green stools, "Sho' can tell this aint no black bar!"

He ordered a blackberry brandy, and the bartender told him they did not carry that brand with the tone of a doctor who has just informed a patient that he has leukemia. Then he turned around and made a wide gesture indicating all the kinds of liquor they did have.

"Damn, I done landed in liquor heaven! What you suggest?" asked Joe.

The bartender looked closely at Joe, intuiting he was a straight man, and suggested Dos Equis. Joe asked what it was and was told it was dark beer. The sleek Spanish bartender laid it down gracefully as if it had just floated there on its own.

Then two handsome, blond, men without shirts came over to asked him to dance. They told him they had seen his Calvin Klein underwear Ad.

And one smiled broadly and said Mr. Joe had a big package.

Joe replied "I aint carried nothin'."

The gays exchanged looks and burst out laughing, and said "Oh, yes, you were. Oh, definitely!"

"I begins to intuit what ya means. Ol' Joe don' roll that way. But he dance like a motherfucker."

The two grabbed him, one on each side and led him to the black and white squared marble dance floor. There was a large crystal ball overhead that sent out red, green, and blue glints over the dance floor.

It was kind of like a too big to carry diamond. Also the stobe lights were going giving all movement a surreal quality.

Joe noticed the gays clearing a place for him in the middle of the dance floor. Old Joe thought, "Oh, what the fuck? I gives a show. Fo' each circumstance, they be a proper action." He took off his shirt, showing his still tight midriff. And he bumped. And he grinded. And generally pretended he was fucking horses up the ass. It was to Gloria Gaynor's, I Will Survive." They clapped and let him pass. If straights can have gaynar, gays can also have the opposite.

When he went back to the bar he ordered something different. Something stronger on the advice of the bartender. It was Salignac and went down like liquid fire. "Blackberry brandy be like Kool-Aid compared to this shit."

"Sir, are you sure you're not gay," said the bartender with a wink.

"Reasonably so, last time I look. God done hard wired me this way," replied Joe, who softened his words with a smile. "It be God's way to make a friend wherever ya goes," he thought.

Then he noticed a pair of long, red, immaculately manicured nails gently grasping his forearm. He followed them to their inception. He saw a pair of beautiful slanted yellow eyes like those of a cougar, a burnt sienna, full, pouty mouth and a face right out of Italian Vogue. She was dressed in a low cut black velvet sheath and silver strappy high heels. He could see the pearlescent mounds of her breasts and the beginnings of her small pink nipples. She was in no way anorexic although dramatically thin.

Mr. Joe thought, "She white but pretty equal to Etta." Her skin had the look of a rare night blooming orchid. He sensed a powerful personality. Her perfume smelled like poisonous flowers growing in a forest primeval. He liked it. He liked her.

"Night things grows inside this woman while Etta be the raw earth. I aint never knowed a woman like this. She the kind to cut ya behind yo' back, so's ya dies real slow. Etta, she cut ya right to yo' face and make it so's ya don' suffer much."

"Dang,"he thought, "I wants to fuck her 'til her teeth falls out."

And he got an immense, obvious, overwhelming hard-on. He wasn't the only one. When they got to the dance floor, Mr. Joe discovered a different reality.

And he thought, "Joe you always been a gentleman, and this 'gal' got feelings, too jes' like anyone else. You gon' damn sure treat her like a lady. Joe, ya understands she be a lady in her heart. She done suffer too much already fo' what she is. You aint gon' make it worse!" Joe held her close and occasionally kissed her cheek, or her ears, and neck, and he was at half mast and hoped that would satisfy "her".

At the end of the night, Marlene asked him to come over. And Mr. Joe prayed to the Lord for inspiration, and it came in a blinding light.

"Listen, Marlene, I aint been 'specially honest wid' ya. I be from the South and we got some things you aint got here in the East. My woman, name of Etta, be a voodoo priestess."

"Joe, that's just shit. There's no such thing! You're just not in to me!"

"In the deep South they aint believe in fairies neither. They think everyone be wild 'bout pussy!"said Joe.

"Oh, Joe, come on. You just don't dig me because I'm the way I am. Straight men always freak out and dump me," interjected Marlene.

"Marlene, if I don' dig ya why I spend all night rubbin' up agin' ya and kissin' ya and shit. Girl, you done turned on Ol' Joe!"

"Well, I did feel something down there," replied Marlene."

See, Gal aint nothin' wrong wit' yo' memory. I tells ya 'bout Etta now. She got the bones to cast fo' the past and the future. And they be human bones. Sometime, and I hates to say this 'bout my Etta, she drink human blood. Etta can feel what Ol' Joe do no matter how far he be. Her mind be linked to my mind and so far, I aint done shit.

She keep jars of people's hearts and rattlesnakes around floating in some godawful liquid jes' to remind people of what she can do. Rumor is fo' the right price, she can raise a dead man. If she get jealous she can jes' reach in and tear out yo' heart from your chest even if you be thousands of miles away. And Etta gone do you too, if ya messes wit' me. I seen her do it. Jes' standin' there with the full heart, blood a pourin' out of her mouth. She got teeth like a wolf and I aint 'zactly sure she be one hundred percent human! But I can say fo' sure she fuck like a goddamned tornado!"

Marlene smiled gently and kissed Old Joe on the cheek, and said, "I believe I've met my first gentleman."

THE WINE TASTING PARTY

On Friday, Mr. Joe had on his thinking cap. "Miz Lucille say I ought to improve my social skills. Like sometime I say jes' what be on my mind and I cusses a bit mo' than I should. She say it be real good I go to Penn but I should get to know the 'right people'. Whatever that mean. My way of thinkin' is that the right people be anyone who don' fuck ya over. She say that aint 'zactly what she mean. She done hand me a ticket to Green Leaf Winery and say my ass be grass if I don' go. I sees it cost two hundred dollars and that I gots to go. No bullshit."

"I bathes and shaves at bathes at Miz Lucilles's and she give me this real fancy shave perfume. I knows it make me smell like a fairy. I puts on my red suit and white shoes wid' matchin' socks. That show ya gots class.

I gets there and it look lie a fuckin' funeral, all them navies, grays, and blacks. I be a cardinal amongst the ravens. I think it be sad they don' know how to dress fo' a party and git they freak-on. They be about fifty of them motherfuckers and they aint say shit to me unless it be 'how ya do'in' or 'nice day aint it. I thinks they be 'fraid I gon' to drags they womins into the bushes and fuck them raw. I can't 'jes make an announcement that this aint be the case.

So I sticks to myself and to one white lady lagin' behind. She be all plump and juicy like a Georgia peach. She don' like them others neither it seem. She got this real high up blond air like Dolly Parton and it look jes' like a bird nest. I drinks the wine and it taste like horse piss, not sweet at all like I likes it. And I notices they swishes it around in they mouths and spits it out like Listerine. I almost passes out from the shock. How they gon' git' they freak-on like this and the motherfucker done cost two hundred dollars! Then I notice the other white lady don' spit out nothin' neither and she give them the finger when they aint lookin', and she smile right at me. It weren't a 'you is a dumb bastard smile.' It were a 'I wants to do ya smile.

'I tries the cheese, I aint know what it were but it sho' meet wid' my approval. And they had these lil' white crackers that be jes' right fo' the cheese. And I thinks to myself, "Jes' what is the sicheeation, Joe?"

I ast her if she from out of town or here, and she say out of town, and leavin' early next thinkin'. This like a thing Ol' Joe can do and Etta never find out and cut off my balls.

She ast what size my shoes be and I replies, "Size thirteen" And she look real close at my large hands and I know what she be thinkin'. She smile real devilish and Ol' Joe rise to the occasion. I also know this aint what Miz Lucille mean by the 'right people'. I know she mean those snotty bastards. Maybe they womins go off somewhere and talk 'bout they shrunkin' lil' twats, and the men be all lyin' bout' size. Ol' Joe aint never lie on this. No need."

I tells her to hold her horses, that we sho' gon' do the do. And I walks over to the other wine spittin' group and says, "Who want to discuss the practice of the philosophy of Nietche in the the Modern World?" They all look like I jes' capped them or done pulled down my pants and took a giant shit. They aint no takers and I thinks, "What the hell, I done give it my best."

Then I thinks on my piece of ass. I needs a good hotel what got cheeseburger take-out, beer, and no damn roaches. The Blue Angel come to mind. It named after Marlene Dietrich, an old timey actress. This lady be as sweet as a vanilla ice cone and tasted just as sweet. And she done up like a Fredericks of Hollywood model with Hot pink corset and pale pink hose with lil' white roses at the top. And the corset push her tits up like two giants mounds of pineapple sherbet.

Usually I jes' goes wid' black womins cuz I knows they heads. With whites, I aint to sure. Maybe she want me to drink champagne out of her shoe or crawl 'round on the flo' and play 'horsie'. Plus not all that long ago, they was lynchin' black mens fo' 'jes lookin' at white girls. That do kind of put a pall on things but not fo' long.

We done all the fuckin' and suckin' possible fo' one night. The next mornin' I sees I done aged her somewhat. I be feelin' I aint want 'nother woman never agin'. Then I thinks of somethin' funny in her name. Mrytle in the girdle. Over all it sho' be worthwhile.

I gits' in the shower and practically uses Brillo Pads to wash off her smell. I shaves like a wall street broker and washes my mouth wid' some tough ass mouth wash.

In the meantime, Etta be up at 6:00 A.M. waitin' fo' me to help wid' the corn huskin' and plantin'. I tells her I be late 'cuz my back be painin' me and it weren't no lie. Etta hand me a giant piece of corn bread and some black coffee. She aint hearin' it. If I was a paraplegic, I still gon' work! No matter what ya gits from a woman, ya gon' pay fo' it some kind of way.

Etta be lookin' fo' sho' like a farm girl wid' her bib over-alls, checkered shirt and timberline boots. From sun up to sun down, we work our damn asses off and the corn husks cut us something fierce. The Etta cook a meal enough to fell a giant. Ham, greens, fried chicken, black-eyes peas, macaroni and cheese, corn on the cob, and biscuits, home made. We have watermelon fo' desert.

Then I rests and sits there listenin' to the rough, sad' ol' spirits of Mississippi blues men. And I channels they spirits. Mr. Joe can do losts of special things but I aint sayin'. Lighten' Hopkins, Muddy Waters, Blind Lemon Jefferson, even Billie comes through. Then Etta turn around from washin' the pots and pans, and kickin' the dog, and I sees she got red glints in her eyes and I knows this aint be good. No kind of way.

She grab my hand roughly and drag me up the stairs like a sack of potatoes. I knows I be in fo' it. Tonight I be like a damn white man who fuck his secretary and can't git' it up fo' his wife! Etta climb on top like she do and I don' rise to the occasion. So she git' off do the next best thing and I tastes her sweet peach like a good man should. But nothin' on my front. It like someone tryin' to be great and missin' the mark totally.

She git' real quiet and soft like a canary in a cage and she say, "Baby, it aint no thang. Everybody miss the mark sometime. I know you aint perfect, Joe. Don' worry, Baby, I still loves ya wid' all my heart." But her face be in darkness, and I thinks on the fact that the devil's face also be in darkness.

Then we spoon up and she wrap herself around me and I feel as warm ginger bread cookies what done jes' come out of the oven. Then around 3:a.m. I be layin' on my back and she be sittin' on my chest' wid' a butcher knife at my throat. I feels little trickles of blood, and I smells liquor powerful strong on her breath. I sees the flash of the whites her eyes and I thinks, "She be in the devil's hands now." My cock rise up like fuckin' Mount Everest or somethin'. When Etta gits hard I gits turned on.

"Tell me who she be, ya fuckin' bastard! What her name and where do she live? Tell me, cocksucker, or I gon' cut yo' damn arteries"

"Etta, Etta. I aint done nothin'. I swears on the Cross, Girl." I figure God gon' let me slide on this one. "Baby, aint no one but you. You is my damn wife only not sanctified!"

She replied, "You aint got no respec' fo' me. Joe. I be jes' a piece of ass to ya', Joe. Like them stank bitches at the Ho' House! One of yo' ho's approach me, the one wid' the orange hair and blue lightenin' streak, and she done call me down. And say, 'she be yo' woman and she gone' kick my damn ass! I got down from my wagon and kick her hard as I could in the stomach. And I pray she be wid' child. Then I pounds her into the red clay that be the road. You see, muscle be tougher than flab, and all she do is lie on her back, take mens, and eat bon bons. Then I cuts her under both breasts, and say mess wid' Joe one mo' time, I gon' cut out yo' fuckin' heart and eat it fo' dinner. Then I leaves her layin' in the middle of the road a'moanin."

"Oh, Baby, you know Joe don' love that cheap bitch. Don' kill Ol' Joe.

I loves ya like I loves the night sky all dancin' wid' silver stars, or the blue wind comin' 'round the corners in spring. I thinks of marigolds when I sees ya, Etta. Partly cuz they aint fancy and they smells of earth jes' like you, Etta. You be the only woman Ol' Joe ever love. Partly because you is scary sometime, and soft like an angel at other times. You is Life, Etta. You gon' scare the shit out of Old Man Death when he comes fo' ya."

""Oh, Joe, you is always so good wit' words, and meltin' my heart. My heart go all soft and I feels some kind of wild when ya talks. All the things I done experienced in my life done made me hard. But when you speaks I thinks of daisies a blowin' and a bendin' in the wind on a green, green hill," said Etta.

"I know, Baby, I know," he said wrapping her in his strong arms. "The Lord done want it this way".

JAIL BAIT

Miz Edna came over to Old Joe in church, offering a large plastic, container of black eyed peas. Her fat hands with multiple rings reminded him of his own mother's hands, "Oh, Miz Edna, you done honored me wid' yo' cookin". He smelled the baby powder coming from her person. She lingered awhile, waiting for her true knight, namely, Mr. Joe. He was a feisty rooster in a hen house with too many hens. And, he thought," I 'jes don' like the smell of old pussy. It stink
like a pile of dead cats. Lord, forgive me," he thought.

Then he wondered why every time the old ladies had him over they always wanted him to fix something. Did he look like a damn plumber or ask them to knit him a damn sweater, or darn his socks?"

Then Miz Hilda and Miz Gracie came over and their brows were knitted together like an over cooked omelet and their purple lips were twisted in a tight line looking like they'd just seen a very graffic. bloody wreck on the freeway.

"Mr. Joe, we got a sitcheeation in our neighborhood. They runnin' young teenage ho's at all hours of the night. F this, and F. that and drugs, coke, MJ. and Heron. And he beat the shit out of them if they don' bring in enough money. He ride round in a yellow Cadillac like he hot shit. And the cops don' care none bout' the black community. Sometimes they on the take," said Miz Hilda.

"He work out of the bus stop wid' the lil' runaways and mail order brides. And he got two big mens to protect him from the other pimps. They so big and ugly they faces looks like road kill. He the one who do the girls and he like it fine. He punch 'em like they was dogs and they people 'jes like anyone else. Maybe he never git' enough of the tit or he be gay," said Miz Gracie.

"Ya gots to do somethin' Mr. Joe. You is our last hope," said Miz Hilda.

"Well, you aint notice I aint made of steel and don' fly, ladies, but I gives it a try. It take some powerful cogitation. Battles aint won by guns; they won by strategy. There be David and Goliath. Guess which one I is?" He patted each plump lady, one cheek and kissed her on the other.

"Ladies, you done got Ol' Joe on yo' side and he gon' kick some pimp ass."

Old Joe went to the neighborhood the following night, identified the pimp, and thought, "Keep yo' friends close and yo' enemies closer."

And he found the yellow Cadillac, and noticed the fine, crisp tailor made shirt sleeve with diamond cuff links trailing down the side of the car. Joe went over to the car and stared into a fine Hispanic face.

He looked like a priest, or somebody's brother. The evil was finely disguised like a basket of vipers. He had soft, moist almond eyes and sharp, very white teeth.

"A pimp vampire, anything be possible."

He could see why the young girls worshiped and trusted him. There was a faint resemblance to a drug store "Jesus." Joe asked him what a blow job cost (twenty-five) and a throw down (fifty). Then he dumped his pockets out and naturally they were empty. He smiled real sheepishly, like a "dumb bastard," and said he would be back at the end of the week with his pay check. Joe also told him, "the brothers" wanted a real big party with all the girls, $5000, down and $ 10,000 at the end. I said that they wanted "freaky shit, S&M, bondage, costumes like cop or French maid."

The pimp replied, "They do it all. I trained them myself. But don't kill them. Too risky. Police involvement, you know, hombre."

Joe stayed around just to get the atmosphere, and he saw a lot of gray haired family men picking up the young fresh flowers and he thought, "I bet in church you done donate a fortune to the collection box, and you buys yo' wife nice dresses, but no way is your fat white ass go'in to heaven."

Joe came back before the specific party on Friday and informed the pimp, Manolo, that he wanted to sample the goods and see if they were worth it. Manolo asked if the big deal was still on, and Joe said, "Sho' don' worry none. The brothers be powerful horny." He requested the one known as "Blondie", and the little red head with the frizzie hair.

Manolo claimed they were his most popular girls as they, at thirteen, were the youngest, "fresh meat, only a slightly spoiled." Joe had a powerful hatred for him and felt that the Lord would justify it in this case. He offered to pay double since he was a black man, and he smiled wide and said, "okay."

The girls both were delighted by this, and Old Joe thought, "The girls be amazin' like out of that book I done read called, Lolita, 'cept they sucks cocks not lollipops. Ol' Joe like the lil' blond one wid' the pigtails tied up in pink ribbons, a pastel green mini skirt, and pink and white stockings like a barber's pole. She got a sweet face too, like she still believe somethin' real good gon' happen. She got a lot of sugar amid the arsenic. I sees the lil' red headed one be all evil wid' the pain the mens done give her. It all she can do to keep from killen' them. Evil fester and fester like a thorn and she gon' need a lot more love and attention than "Blondie" to git' right."

He told them he had a "father fixation" and was taking them to the Dairy Queen and a movie and nothing else. They exchanged glances and he surmised they thought he was going to bounce them on his knee, and reach under their skirts. When they saw it wasn't the case their faces lit up like they were Bill Gates's kids on Christmas morning. Then he told them they were going to party with some really rich black athletes on Friday coming and that there would be no "damn freaky shit."

Blondie, ducked her head, and said, "Is it true what they say about black men?" And she giggled like a little girl.

"Blondie, I gon' count on you to tell the rest of the girls they gon' to be a big party wid' all of you girls this Saturday comin' They be rich black athletes. The trip gon' be real long and y'al gon' have plenty chilled champagne and all the fancy cheese whut cost an arm and a leg. All ya can eat. Smile for Ol' Joe, Blondie." And she did.

Then Joe devised his plan. Get rid of the soldiers first, the Rotweilers, secure the girls, and deal with the pimp last. The soldiers, who were also working the door of a sleazy club, were ex-cons who were dealing drugs to the clientele. He located their parole officers and made the necessary call. "What they git' fo' not being college boys! Dumb asses!" he thought. "Why they aint figure someone gon' turn them in, I aint never know. Ya doesn't have to be no Einstein to figure it out."

He rolled into the pimp's territory on Friday, as promised and gave him, the promised, $5000. The pimp's eye's were darting about and he had the look of a cow on the slaughtering block. Joe had a large, well armored truck stocked full of amazing delicacies. Joe drove and knew there would be no party. If he had had the pimp arrested, they would have only gone to another pimp. These girls, he knew had been raped and abused by their own fathers and sought other men just like them. They looked on their pimps as their protectors, their lovers, their friends. He was taking them to a lock down facility run by nuns in Cheyenne, Pennsylvania.

Only these nuns wore camaflage pants and army boots and knew more about these girls than they knew themselves. There was no smiling, no warmth from the nuns. They were there to learn trades, like office and computer skills, carpentry, plumbing, heating, and refrigeration. In some cases, college prep. The nuns never wavered in their attitudes and were roundly despised. They knew the girls only understood harsh treatment, and that's what they gave them.

Old Joe explained the facility to the "church" ladies and one thing in particular. "They has this man, Father Shea, who pries open they diseased, shattered lil' hearts wid' the ease and gentleness of an angel. He hold them when they cries and deflects they bitterness towards men.

He say, ' Let no man ever hurt you again, Darlin'. You see a distortion. An evil sickness. Evil has made you sick like a poison. You are Somebody! Quit suffering and start to live!" And they cries and cries in his arms. "Good done hurt you same as evil when ya first gits' it. All they ever knowed was was evil and the Good Father know this. He gone break them like fine crystal and put them back together. He put them back real slow. And gentle like when ya holds a baby bird in 'yo hands. He gone make them too tough and too dangerous fo' any pimp. And the last day when they graduates, the nuns gone be all laughin' and singin' like a pack of blue jays whut been released from they cages.

Then they gone know the truth. That how it gone go down, ladies. I seen it work fo' other po' souls. It work sure good this time, I'm thinkin'. Now I gots one mo' thing to do. Slay the dragon. Ladies y'al know Ol' Joe weren't always 'wid the Lord. I ast the Lord fo' one special prayer. It go:

Bring it back, Lord.
That I may do whut I got to do.
Tonight, I walks in the devil's shoes.
Forgive me, O, Lord."

"You aint kill him, Mr. Joe," said Miz Gracie in dismay.

"I gone do my dead level best not to, Gal. I gone use some ol' down home persuasion. Don' you worry none."

That night he convinced Manolo to "ride" him home since they were "bidness partners." On the way over they passed Miz Lucille's house, and Manolo grabbed his cock and winked at Joe as they passed by her home.

"It aint even that way, SOB. This aint no Scarlet O'Hara and field hand thing." Then in the darkness he reached over quick as a flash and sliced off Manolo's ear. "Lissen' Van Gogh, you aint never come this way agin' or I gone make you a fuckin' soprano. Tonight, I done save a hundred souls fo' the misfortune of one."

MERRY CHRISTMAS, MR. JOE

"Mr. Joe, you aint got the class to go," said Jaquita, in her work clothes, a Ralph Lauren ensemble and Jimmy shoes.

"Sho', I does. I knows all the presidents and whut they done since day one. Clinton be my favorite. He done whut any black man woulda done only he 'git caught."

"Mr. Joe you are just nasty to think on it," replied Jaquita.

"It aint nasty, Gal. It be natural. Why is you talkin' all white and shit?"

"I'm switching up, Mr. Joe, and so should you. The first time you say aint, they'll lynch you!"

"Oh, Gal, people aint that mean."

"What kind of world do you think we're living in? My own mother would put me out if she knew I was gay."

"Gal, everybody know you gay wid' yo' cut off blue jean jacket, camaflage pants, yo' no makeup and ass turned around baseball cap! Does ya think ya gots to suck pussy on the church front lawn fo' them to know?"

"Mr. Joe, you are uneducated, crude, and without any semblance of manners," retorted Jaquita.

"Gal, ya talks one kind of way and be's another."

"If you had the sense God gave a gnat, you'd do the same. It makes white people think you're smarter, on a par with them. You get their respect. And by the way, are you going as Santa?"

"You done know Ol' Joe, Gal."

"Oh, God, at a white party. Why don't you just go as Uncle Remus and set the black race back to Jim Crow?"

"I don' know whut you is drivin' at but I aint like it none. My friend, Miz Lucille, think it be a good idea to show that Santa can be any color."

"Is Miss Lucille white and a complete imbecile?"

"Yes to the first, no to the second," replied Mr. Joe.

"Mr. Joe they will kill you. They're expecting a white Santa."

"I 'specs I take a few of 'em 'wid me, then."

"Mr. Joe, do not, I repeat, do not under any circumstance give them THE WORD."

"And who don' want THE WORD?" exclaimed Mr. Joe.

"Atheists, people who worship nature, Wiccans. I don't know. Take your pick," replied Jaquita.

"That do seem a tad odd since it were God, Hisself, who created nature. Look at cells, cows, lightening, and prize fighters. And Degas, the guy who paint all them pretty 'lil ballerinas. Aint that proof enuff fo' you, Jaquita or do He have to come to 'yo bedside at night and recite, 'Ode to Jaquita?"

"Mr. Joe, these are white people. For Christ's sake! Is she Italian by any chance?

"Sho' and she look like a fuckin' movie star."

"You're in for a big surprise, Mr. Joe."

"What they gone have spaghetti and meat balls. Chef Boyardee?"

"You'll see, Mr. Joe, and rent a fat suit. They like their Santas very rotund."

"Don' ya think Ol' Joe know what Santa look like. I be one jolly motherfucker!"

On Christmas Eve, Miz Lucille opened the door and upon seeing Old Joe, her entire face lit up. To look at Joe was to perceive "Santa": she saw it in his old eyes. The power for good, the loving heart, the empathy for the sacred wishes of little children. She knew this came from experiencing a lot of pain and disappointment. Good is a power and a radiance. Miz Lucille wore a long silver lame evening sheath slit up the sides. Her thin shoulders reminded him of the wings of a sparrow fallen from a tree. Her glorious platinum hair fell down her back like an avalanche of winter snow. Her indigo eyes, were long lashed, powerful, and intensely kind, the kind of eyes that linger in the mind of the beholder.

Mr. Joe thought, "Dang, this be the finest white woman I ever seen. Them long legs goes right up to her ass. She be like white crystal, all glowing like an angel, and too easy to break. My bitch, Etta, be more like the earth. I picks the land over the angels, cuz an angel break too easily. I needs a woman whut can hate, and love like all hell fire! Miz Lucille break into a million little pieces and never go back together.

Mr. Joe had an observation about the music in general, and Handel's Messiah, in particular. "Dang," the thought, "aint this jes' like white people. Don' know how to git' they freak on. What this shit, 'eggnog'. Taste like a damn Dairy Queen milk shake. Where the Jack Daniels and coke. And the music. Aint nobody dead yet but it do seem that way. Why aint they playin' real Christmas music? Lou Rawls, Ella, Lena, Louie Armstrong. Anything!"

Mr. Joe prided himself on his "class" for not saying what he was thinking.

Miz Lucille walked him through the party introducing him simply as "Santa". He saw the looks on the faces of the adults and knew what they were thinking but were too polite to say. The little children had no such reservations. They wanted to know why Santa was black. Miz Lucille fielded the question deftly.

"As you know, children, Santa is magical and can do anything. If he wants to be white, he can. If he wants to be black, he can. It's who he is inside that makes him Santa. Sometimes he changes skin color so all children, both black and white, can experience the joy of Christmas. If you don't believe he is Santa, just look in his eyes."

Each child, one by one, looked in his old eyes, and saw the honeyed warmth and innocence. He was someone who believed in dreams, ice castles floating in the sky, reindeer hooves prancing in air, and stockings full of unearthly delights. He believed in these things because he never had them. He knew what it was like to want, and want, and want, until it became a surgeon's scapel slicing the heart. He sat down and began to listen to their tiny, fragile dreams, and immense material desires.

Toward the end a little red haired haired girl came and sat on Old Joe's lap and her eyes were brimming with tears.

"Whatsa matter, honey. yo' mommy can't buy you yo' favrite' dolly?" he asked.

"No, Santa. Mommy's going to die and they can't make her well. Can you cure my mommy?"

"Baby, ol' Santa aint no doctor and he aint God. Is ya sure she aint gone make it, baby?"

"Yes, Santa. It's leukemia."

"That be real sad, baby," he said, putting his arms around her. "She gone go to heaven, honey, and be wid' God. He take care of all the good folks and give them what the always be wantin'. God have sway over this sad ol' earth, and he gone give her books, and music, and pretty pictures and he gone let her go right on lovin' you."

"But, she's leaving me forever and ever," said the girl, tears streaming down her face.

"I tell ya she aint never leave ya and always be lookin' down on ya. Like when ya graduates college or gits' married. And ya gone feel her hand touchin' ya every day in the warmth of the mornin' sun. Ya 'blieve Ol' Santa, baby.?"

The little girl nodded and gave Joe a wan smile. He knew he could only lessen her pain and not vanquish it entirely. He wondered why more pimps, psychos, and murderers did not get cancer. And then thought, "I aint never understand the Lord. I jes' does his bidding as best I can."

Then Joe decided to put some life into the party by discussing Flannery O'Connor's story the "Artificial Niggar." A boy and his uncle wander into the wrong end of town and the boy accidentally trips over a black lady's leg injuring her slightly, and his own uncle pretends not to know him. This, of course, angers the boy. On their way back they see an Uncle Tom type lawn ornament and call it "the artificial niggar."

"They done thought we was going to boil them alive or some shit! And how you like the word, artificial," said Joe.

A man, who looked like a newscaster evinced the theory that that could never happen in modern times due to a more informed populace and to affirmative action. According to him, any educated man could advance himself. Joe stated he was not an educated man, and the man replied that there were lots of blue collar jobs, like janitor, dishwasher, clerk, and the like for those truly enterprising souls. Joe noted that the white people were acting like he'd just jacked off on the Oriental carpets.

Then Joe laughed out loud, and said, "Don' worry 'bout Ol' Knucklehead Joe. I made one hundred thousand last year fo' my Calving Klein underwear ads and aint et no canned soup in a month of Sundays!"

The women glanced furtively at his crotch, and the men moved closer to their wives. He noted how "a black bitch aint do no lookin'. Jes' come right over, put her hand on it, and say let's 'git it on." He further thought, "They lucky I aint start on that fucker Nietche! I can go on fo' days 'bout that motherfucker!"

As they headed for the dinner table Joe realized his stomach was underprivileged and he would be willing to "eat the ass end out of a billy goat". Then he found out things were not what he had expected. It was not the traditional turkey and stuffing dinner.

Joe thought to himself:

"They got these seven fishes, and none like a man like, fried. Fish got to be fried to taste good. I aint never had nothin' but whiting or catfish. Actually, in truth, a man only like a rare steak, and his woman the same way. I eats this shit, and it go down like pieces of raw liver, and I be smiling like a fox in a hen house. They got these weird ass vegetables I aint never seen befo' all fried in olive oil. And fucked up twisty bread with hard crust like I break my damn teeth or some shit. And I eats they fucked up deserts, name of tiramisu and cannoli. Then they breaks out the wine and it be sweet jes' like I likes it.

Then fo' no reason the words, The Last Supper, comes to me. Oh, Lord, no!"

Mr. Joe completed the meal and gave Miz Lucille his one special Christmas gift. He asked her for the recipes for all "that horrible shit."

And she lit up like she was the only woman who could turn Favio straight.

Around eleven when he reached home, he found Jaquita waiting for him completely saying nothing. She merely took his hand and said, "Come on, Mr. Joe, we gone eat."

ARNETTA

It was about eleven and Arnetta was knocking on Miz Lucille's door to talk to Mr. Joe. She knew Miz Lucille would be at the club. Mr. Joe came to the door with a crusting of sleep in his eyes, and a big yawn.

"Dang, Gal, I aint seen ya in a month of Sundays. How the hell is ya?"

"It's important, Mr. Joe, said Arnetta, she was a six foot, one inch drag queen. She was a black transsexual hooker. She had no pimp because she was too smart for that, and also because she used to be a man. Also she could be quite violent as some foolish pimps had found out. Her long gold nails were not just purely decorative and her punch could knock a man into Sunday. She also carried a small revolver in her gold sequined pocket book and was not afraid to use it.

"Mr. Joe, this is 'bout Aimee, one of the working girls, and a heron junkie. We gots ta git' her children away from her some kind of way. Social workers keep givin' em' back. You know, preserve the fambly unit. It's horseshit, Mr. Joe. She got lil' Erline, her 'leven year old out their turnin' tricks wid' her to git' her damn fixes. It be horrible, Mr. Joe." Her beautiful, haunting, almond colored eyes spilled over with tears.

Mr. Joe told her to come in and sit down, and he poured her a shot of blackberry brandy, which she threw back immediately, and made the gesture for a refill. Arnetta has a special place in Old Joe's heart.

For a rough, tough, nasty street hooker she had very soft, sweet, heart.

If a girl was bleeding in the street, it was Arnetta who held her in her arms, and called the ambulance. It was also Arnetta who chastised the pimp. Arnetta had very rough, pocked skin and was usually heavily made up but her face was striking and dangerously beautiful. Her body was thin and elegant. Her eyes glowed yellow brown like the eyes of a cougar. She usually wore sequined or see through clothes with thigh high black vinyl high heeled boots. She did not lack for clients. She did not use drugs and disapproved of those who did.

Arnetta slammed down the shot glass and gestured for yet another. Then the tears just streamed down her beautiful face. "It aint helpin', Mr. Joe. The pain be so intense I feels like a got a goddamned knife turnin' in my goddamned heart. I can't stand it when innocent children be sufferin'. My own daddy done be since I was nine 'til I leave home. I keeps turnin' in that bitch, Aimee, and they keeps givin' em back from they foster homes. She evil when she high and beat 'em somethin' fierce. She got three of 'em' , two, nine, and 'leven (the girl, Erline). She gits out of rehab, smilin' like Cinderella and they believes she okay.

When they gone wake up? When she kill one of em'? She broke that baby's arm, say he fell out of a chair. They all got these bruises big time. Joe, I can't bear to see this shit. Some people say I go'in to hell fo' what I does, but Joe you done know me. You know I aint no hard hearted bitch. I 'fraid if she don' stop this shit, I goes over there and wastes her myself! I aint playin', Mr. Joe."

"I know you aint, Baby," said Old Joe. He reached in his pocket and handed the two thousand dollars and told her to get out of town for a couple of months, and said, "Ol' Joe got this one, Arnetta, ya hear?"

"Dang, Mr. Joe, where ya gits that kind of money?"

"Ol' Joe got it go'in on, Baby," he said.

Then Arnetta said, "Who protect my girls when I gone?"

"Me and the some brothers I knows can pay 'em a visit. These brothers done some hard time for what I aint sayin. But it scare the shit out of them pimps. See, pimps is all ' bout fuckin' over womins but they 'fraid of mens."

At three o'clock, Christmas day, he paid Aimee a visit. His breath froze in the air and he felt like icicles were forming in his heart. He pounded and pounded on the door. Finally, the eleven year old girl, Erline, answered. She fixed her lips in a practiced, fake, mockery of seduction as if her were going to perform a sexual act on him. She was a blond, pleasant looking child with too much rouge on her cheeks and vivid turquoise eye shadow.. The makeup was so grotesques as to remind one of the movie. "Bride of Chucky."

"No, Baby, it aint that way. Joe be here to see yo' mama?"

She flashed him her most sexual look. As she walked she swung her ass in a seductive, adult way, as if to say, "Young meat, only slightly soiled."

Old Joe took the time to look over the apartment. Dirty "hooker"clothes were strewn all over the worn, sodden couches and box containers of Chinese and MacDonalds rested on the cheap, Formica breakfast table. Elvis Pressley's, "Blue Christmas" was playing on the CD, and Joe thought, "That be the goddamned truth!"

The baby was sitting in a soiled diaper in the middle of the living room floor, and its eyes were vacant and staring. It was the look of a child who had cried itself silent and lost the hope of getting any attention or love. The nine year old was sitting on the dirty couch seemingly mesmerized by a cartoon show and drinking orange soda, and eating popcorn. He did not acknowledge Old Joe. Joe knew he had lost faith in the prospect of getting any sane, loving behavior from any adult. Joe noted the numerous bruises on his arms, and he knew the most painful bruise was inside, on his poor, young heart. Upon inspecting the refrigerator, he saw about four pieces of old bologna, a half carton of velveeta cheese and a loaf of white bread. More numerous were the beer cans, possibly two cases.

He went over to the boy and handed him two hundred dollars with the suggestion for him to hide the money from his mother and use it to buy food. He said, "If yo' mama notice ya gots a lil' money ya tells her ya got it from a special male friend and he be too 'shamed ta meet her."

"What do I have to do for you, mister?"

"Nothin', child. Just try to have a good Christmas and git' somethin'nice." Joe noticed his hair was bright red like "Opey on the old Andy Griffith show. His cowlick seemed so sweet and vulnerable that Joe placed a hand lightly on the tops of the boy's head. The child cringed and moved away. Old Joe just said, "It's okay, Baby, I understand. Ol' Joe done 'pologize."

Joe, still waiting, began to look around at the Christmas decorations. There was a silver artificial tree, that turned around and had various lights shine on it, and a garish, plastic manger scene with a Madonna looking grotesquely cheap on the fake fireplace mantel. It was if the devil had vomited up this Christmas from the depths of his bowels. Even, the song, Jingle Bells, sounded hollow and ominous. A palpable sadness hung in the air.

Aimee appeared after about forty minutes, dressed in a revealing black sheath and silver strap shoes. She looked like a fifties Vargas calendar girl, or a ruined version of Marilyn Monroe. Her soft, blond tousled hair was styled in a fifties way, and she had vapid, even, pretty features like a beauty queen from the Midwest. Her figure was voluptuous on a small scale, clearly not someone who would go to the gym. Joe thought, "Somethin' evil like dry rot here, empty like a sugar angel on top of a Christmas tree. Sometime evil glow like an emerald and cut like one too."

She said, "I don't' usually entertain at home, but for $250, we can get it on, or $750, for the entire night." Then she winked, and cutely said, "I give a great breakfast."

"I be sure that be the crownin' glory of my life, but I got other bidness wid' you," replied old Joe.

"Whatcha mean" Are you my new social worker? I'm not due for a visit yet."

"I aint no social worker. I here to talk to you 'bout the bidness of yo' soul," replied Joe.

"My soul?" she laughed and threw back her empty blond head. "You're just some crazy religious fuck. Want to do it on the altar? It'll cost a damn site more!" she said.

Old Joe looked at her sternly and said evenly," I aint want yo' damned, ruined white ass, bitch. I "spec you gon' to lissen to Old Joe cuz I don' play. You been beatin' yo' po' lil' kids and ya gots the oldest workin' the streets. No damn food in the fridge and the place a pig sty!"

"Did that fuckin' black bitch, Arnetta send ya? She's always callin' on me like I'm some kind of damned monster!" shouted Aimee.

"Lissen, Miz Arnetta be my friend, and a far, far better person than you'll ever be!"

intoned Mr. Joe. "As fo' you be'in a monster, that be perfectly accurate."

"Miz Arnetta, that's rich. She's a drag queen! A faggot!"

"Bitch, Arnetta be more woman than you'll ever be in yo' whole natural life. You aint got no damned heart!" exclaimed Mr. Joe.

"Who do you think you are, you old niggar. Go shine some shoes and get the fuck out of here before I call the police!" said Aimee.

"I spec' you don' want to do that. The po-lice don' look favorably on those whut got contraband in they houses. Besides, how many black ho's on the street git' pissed maybe and maybe stick a knife in yo' damned back. But it aint no thang." said Joe casually.

"Get out of my fucking house," she screamed. And hold Joe backed her into the wall pinning both her arms.

"Lissen, bitch, and lissen good," Mr. Joe hissed. "I aint no white social worker who believe in the redemption of fuckin ho's souls. How many times ya been to rehab, three, six. Sixty goddamned times. You aaint mean it. You is jes' bull shittin' and you don' love yo' po' lil' children!"

"Ya proves every time ya sticks that fuckin' needle in yo' arm? Ya love heron. You can fool whitie wid' this keep the fambly' together shit but that don' play wid' Ol' Joe."

"I'll file an assault charge against you, you crazy bastard if you ever come here again!" Aimee.

"As I done said befo' how many black ho's can shove a knife in yo' back, or maybe ya likes 'em to cut yo' face wid' they straight edges or does ya think they carries they pocket books jes' fo' the lipstick. Think on it, Gal." Then he released her and he saw ghosts of fear floating in her eyes.

Joe stepped closer and whispered softly in her ear. "This gon' be how it gon' go down. First ya git's yo' lil' gal off the streets. Git' clean yerself. Enroll in some college courses, office maybe. Fill that fridge wid' food and clean this fucking place. Don' fuck up, missie. I be back in two months. Is you clear on this. Don' call the po-lice or nothin'. Or I'll have 'em drop ya on the street!" I don' spec' ya can quit The Life right away. I know ya gots to have yo' money. But, Honey, move towards the light. You is fuckin' wit' the Devil!" Then he left quietly.

Aimee nodded quietly and when he had left she collapsed on her bead and broke down in tears. She felt sour bile rising in her mouth and she flew to the bathroom and vomited up what was left in her stomach from breakfast. Then she looked into her mirror accurately for the first time.

She saw beyond her vapid prettiness. She saw hardness, and sloth, and a brittle coldness. She had not loved herself nor anyone else in her entire life. She knew Old Joe was right. She didn't love them more than she loved getting high. In fact, maybe she didn't love them at all. She crawled back into bed and pulled up the covers.

First she took her oldest, Erline, off the streets. She cleaned the house until it was pristine, filled the refrigerator hugely, and tried to make herself emotionally available to her children. They reacted as if she were a rattlesnake about to strike. They were terrified. They were hurt. They did not believe. She went to her bed room closed the door and shot up. The tears evaporated on her cheeks and her eyes grew dull.

In the weeks following she did all things but one. The need for the drug was just so overwhelming, she could not stop. She needed the hazy, warm, vagueness to deal with her harsh, dangerous life. She continued to try to reach her children who were still unbelieving. She found she could not comprehend course material and had to drop out. One more dream ripped from her heart. Her children, so sad, so very sad.

The social worker came over and looked at the pristine house, the full refrigerator, no bruises, and opened school books. Social workers do not perceive souls as old black men can. She left with a "Crest" smile on her face. She was just the "best" social worker on the whole planet.

Aimee knew Joe would come the next day and he would know the truth. She was too hurt to cry, and she waited. He came in the late afternoon and just stood quietly waiting for her to talk in the kitchen. Then, she ran into his arms and he held her as she sobbed. "You know, don't you, Mr. Joe?"

"Yes, Baby, I know." And he kept holding her. "Lissen, Baby, I know ya done tried powerful much but aint able to quit the horse. "

"I'm just not a mother. You knew that the first time you met me, didn't ya, Mr. Joe? I've ruined them and myself. And I can't even do the college courses."

"Lissen, Baby, this gon' hurt a bit but this what we gon' do. They aint gon' be no white social worker involvement. Them foster homes fucks up the children. We gon' move on everything today. I got a place somewheres for the kids. She a black lady, sweet, and fat, she love the hell out of kids and she cook her ass off and she good wit' helpin' em' wit' school. It aint even in this state. Kids is her life's work and she do get paid fo' it so's she can git' em' things. I got a bus ticket to Syracuse, and a place to stay and a simple kind of job for ya. It aint be rocket science. I hopes, Baby, ya can find the strength to leave The Life cuz God love ya and Ol' Joe love ya. And the hard thing be fo' you ta love you."

Aimee bent over double in pain, and for the first time she knew she loved her children desperately. She cried and went over to them hugging their stiff, resistant bodies, and their eyes began to tear up.

"Oh, my babies, I love you so much. I know I didn't show it. I was so evil," and the dam of her heart burst open.

The little red headed boy, replied sweetly, "We'll miss you, mommy."

The older girl, through her tears, said," You didn't do anything wrong, mommy. You were just trying to take care of us."

Then Mr. Joe said, "You youngsters kiss yo' mommy now. And then ya gits' yo' favorite books, toys and stuff. And ya gits right in the van outside. Ya don' need anythin' else. Do it right now."

He turned to Aimee and said, "Ya gots to leave right away befo' the memories kill yo' po' lil' heart, Baby. Ya done a wonderful thing, Miz Aimee. Puttin' someone else befo' yerself. Real brave and true and ya aint the bad person ya thought ya was."

"I think God got a place in Heaven fo' junkies wit' good hearts.

DEATH WILL BE NO MORE

Mr. Joe looked out on the gray sky and hard sleet from his cabin, and thought, "Stormy Monday, and Tuesday look jes' the same." He took a swig of blackberry brandy from his silver flask and brought out his harmonica. "I gon' summon out the ol' blues men, and bring they souls in line wid' mine. Do some channelin'. This sho' be the day fo' it. Then I gon' git me some grits and eggs and black coffee from the HoJo down the way."

The world was gray from ass to toe, "make a body want to git drunk," thought Joe. The he saw something yellow approaching from the mist.

"Look like a goddamned Smiley face," he mused.

As the figure got closer, he saw it was the Reverend, Wes Brown from Just Wishing and Full of Hope Baptist Church at 50th and Pine. He was wearing a yellow slicker and hat. "No, Chiquita Banana, and forgive me, Lord. You know Ol' Joe aint worth a damn widout his mornin' coffee."

The Reverend stepped up on Joe's porch, such as it was, and shook off the rain water. Joe took one look at his face and thought, "This aint 'bout stiffin' no collection box, or singin' off key in choir. Bound to be 'bout fuckin' out of wedlock, fo' sho'."

"What up, Pastor Wes?" asked Joe.

"Joe, I done come from Miz Edna's and she diein'. She got the lung cancer and aint gone last the night. She be astin' fo' ya, Joe and I done give her Last Rites. She cryin' powerful bad and the machine aint give her no relief no mo'. Can ya come, straightaway, Joe?"

"Why she aint tell no one she sick befo' Rev?" asked Joe

"Cuz she don' want nobody to know her troubles. She aint got nobody to do fo' her, Joe. No husband and no chillen'."

"Sho' I done notice she have the devil's on time catchin' her breath and I ast her and she say she got the asthma," said Joe.

"She proud, Joe. She aint want anyone know her troubles," said the "Rev."

"This be jes' plain tragic. What I got to tell her, Rev?" asked Joe.

"I 'spec that be up to you, Joe. She say you be knowin' jes' what to do."

"I got my old wooden Cross whut I carved and my ol' Bible. The pages kind of yellow but a body can still read 'em."

The "Rev" reached out and put a hand on Old Joes shoulder. "I 'spec ya knows just what to say, Joe. Ya got a way 'bout ya."

"I wished I had yo' confidence but I gon do my damndest," replied Joe.

The "Rev" offered to "ride" Joe over and he accepted. First, though, Joe requested to stop at two places, the grocery store and the liquor store. In the grocery store, he bought a chocolate cake and some ice cream, and a dozen white roses.

At the liquor store, Joe bought a bottle of Pink Zinfandel, thinking to himself, "If it be pink and sweet, a lady gon' like it, fo' sho."

The "Rev" commented, "Ya really think she want the drink, Joe?"

"Rev, on the day a body die he want chocolate, somethin' to drink maybe even a fuck, excuse my French."

"Joe, you aint considerin'…" said the Pastor.

"Depend on whut Miz Edna want, Rev. She got The Word from you, maybe she want whut only a good man can give her now. If so, Ol' Joe gone to send her to heaven wid' a smile on her face. Whatever it take."

"Rev, you tell Etta I aint be back but late or mornin'. She gon' understand. My Etta rough but she good in her heart."

They reached Miz Edna's house and it looked like house out of the Grimm's Fairy Tale, Hansel and Gretel, all trellises and pansies and a panopoly of ceramic cats, elves, and angels. Old Joe entered the house and noticed the rancid stench of approaching death. He opened some of the windows to let the sound and smell of rain permeate the rooms.

"Is that you, Mr. Joe or the damned old Angel of Death?" Miz Edna softly.

"It be Ol' Joe, Miz Edna. I don' kicked that motherfucker's ass right out the back do'!"

He went into her bedroom and was shocked. It looked like she had lost about thirty pounds and there were deep, purple circles under her eyes, and her mouth was twisted in pain. There was a blue tinge to her skin. She had the oxygen machine on and was still struggling to breathe. She noticed one of her breasts was exposed and started to apologize.

"Shh, Baby, aint no need to stand on ceremony. Joe love to see a lovely woman's breast here in this world, and hopefully in the next."

"Oh, Mr. Joe, ya really mean that?"

"Sho', Baby. If Ol' Joe aint never met Etta, he done make you his sweetie pie. Aint ya know that, honey?" he replied.

"Oh, Joe, you is so sweet," she replied.

"No, Baby, I be a motherfucker who know a fine woman when he see one. Now where ya got a vase? I brung ya them white roses."

"Oh, they be my favorite. Forty year ago when I wedded my Henry, they was my bridal bouquet."

"How long yo' man be gone, Miz Edna?" asked Mr. Joe gently.

"Twenty year ago, and I feels like it was just yesterday, Mr. Joe. He done die on me on Christmas of eighty six." And she started to tear up.

Mr. Joe sat on the side of her bed and wiped the tears from her eyes with his large, rough hand.

"Baby, tonight Ol' Joe be yo' man. He done secretly want you fo' a long time."

"Can ya be my husband fo' jes' tonight, Joe?" she asked.

"Sho' Baby. Anythin' ya wants," he replied.

"And Etta aint come to cut me?"

"You don' worry none. Etta understand things like this. Look, honey, I brung ya chocolate cake, butter brickle ice cream and Pink Zinfandel. We gon' party hearty."

"And, what else, Mr. Joe?" she asked with the trace of a smile.

"We gon' make make love like Adam and Eve, Girl!"

"Mr. Joe you is nasty," giggled Miz Edna. Her face began to flush.

"That aint even the half of it," he replied. "Gal, I is filthy!"

She hid her smile behind her hand and the fear fell from her eyes.

"Mr. Joe, can ya hand me my perfume on the dresser?"

"Damn, woman, you done know me. Evenin' in Paris be my favorite! Now when I gits it, I wants you to tell all 'bout yo' life, yo' happiness, yo' sorrows and even the in between times. Don' leave nothin' out, my precious lil' bride. Now where yo' wine glasses so's we can git our drink on. Tell me special 'bout yo' Christmases. Honey, Ol' Joe aint never git enough of you!" he exclaimed.

"Oh, Joe you is so sweet."

"No. I aint. I jes' be enchanted wid' a fine woman."

She told him of her life, spilled its contents out like confetti from a top hat. Then a look of worry came across her face, and she said, "Joe, I got a real bad feelin' I aint go'in to heaven."

"Why, Miz Edna," asked Joe.

"The sin of Envy, Mr. Joe. I jes' hates them skinny, pizza eatin' young gals who can shove any damn thing down they throats, some of which aint even food. And me, and my big self, can't eat hardly nothin'."

"Gal, ya don' worry none. Even Venus de Milo got her arms tore off fightin' wid' 'nother bitch for jes' that reason. All womins got the envy. Aint enough room in heaven fo' all of y'al. He gon' let ya slide."

Miz Edna smiled like an orange sunrise, and further stated, "Mr. Joe, I 'shamed to admit this, but I aint completely like the idea of heaven. Harp music, long white robes, angel food cake and do'in nothin' but praisin' the Lord all day long. I mean some of the time, be okay, or most of the time, but not all of the time..."

"Chile, that be heaven fo' white folk. God, He understand black folk. He know we aint eat no angel food cake. It gon' be soul food, grits, black eyed peas, and shit, and no harp music. It gon' be B.B. King, Muddy Waters, Charlie Bird Parker, Billie, and Ella. Whatever ya wants. And our Lord, He know aint no black folk whut can go widout sex. The white man can but a brother aint never do this. You gon' have one husband, or maybe two, if ya wants it. Denzel, Morgan when they dies. Hell, even Bobby Seale if he dead. God know that black folk do some extra sufferin' while they on this earth and he try to make it up to us!"

"The Rev aint never say that, Mr. Joe."

"That cuz he give you his professional opinion, Miz Edna. I be givin' ya the layman's opinion," replied Joe.

Then she said, "Joe, I feels a quickening in my body. Take me now."

And he did with the ease of the sky kissing the earth.

She sighed and then lay still. Joe took off his old tarnished ring and placed it on her hand and said, "Darlin', wid this ring, I Thee wed."

Her eyes overflowed with tears and she whispered, "Joe."

Then she was still. And he knew. He laid one white rose across her bosom, kissed her on the brow and called the pastor.

Then he knelt by her bedside and said a prayer. It was:

Death will be no more,
Nor crying, nor tears, nor pain.
Because the former things
Have past away.

OLD JOE HOLDS FORTH

Old Joe was sitting in his philosophy class at Penn observing the wealthy students in his class. He did not envy them, he liked them and sometimes socialized with them. It was a real sight to see Old Joe at a "frat" party quaffing green beer on St. Patrick's day. At this moment, He was wondering why white girls often wore their hair straight, parted down the middle, and no make-up. "It don't do nothin' fo' 'em," he thought. "A black gal really know how to do "the do". But some ways a lil' white gal got mo' in her head. But on the other hand, Sister Maya Angelou can write her ass off."

Then the "Prof" began to discuss the philosophy of Nietche, and the concept of the Super Man, a man completely unbound by the rules of society, subject to no moral code or law. Joe was very popular with the students and welcomed by staff as his presence in any class generally increased enrollment. On this particular day, the "Prof" noticed Old Joe's red face, and looking like an Old Testament Moses, only black.

The "Prof" decided it more expedient to just ignore Old Joe.

But Joe was not having it. He broke in, speaking like a Baptist minister, or the late, great Martin Luther King. "How you gon' say somethin' so damn evil, Prof? You ruinin' they young minds! Ya jes' go to North Philly and you gon' see the Super Man. Them bloods caps ya if ya jes' looks sideways at em"! How 'bout' Hitler, Caligula, Al Capone and that Fucker, name of Heidnick! Aint no way he didn't think he were a Super Man to do all that fucked up shit he did. Nietche aint jes' a philosophy; it be a practice! It be the opposite of Christianity, the one true thing in this world!"

Then Old Joe gasped really loud, and fell into the aisle. Then he thought, "This fucker Nietche tryin' to kill Ol' Joe." Then he passed out and woke up in the hospital.

After waking he thought, "I sho' aint be in heaven. Aint no soul food, blackberry brandy, or poontang here!" He asked the blond, attractive, overly starched nurse if it was "serious". She replied that he had experienced a mild "hysteria" attack.

"Is you callin' me a woman?" he queried.

"Decidedly not," she replied archly.

Then Joe further commented on the hospital cuisine. "What the hell is this, lemon jello and beef juice? This aint no meal fo' a man. Does I look like a damn plant to you? Photosynthesis, or some shit?"

"You'll get solid food tomorrow. We just have to run some tests."

Then she handed him a black men's magazine, and said, "Here, we wouldn't want you to lose the use of your limbs while you're in here."

He laughed and said, "Girl, you okay. What yo' name, Baby?"

"Cathy," she replied.

"I aint never knowed a Cathy befo' 'cept fo' Catherine the Great. I hear she like horses powerful much."

"Sir, you are a pill. Do you know I'm the charge nurse? She bent slightly over to his ear, and whispered, "Don't fuck with me, Sir."

"Dang, is you sho' you aint black?" said Joe.

""Reasaonably so.. And Sir. Don't do anything rash while you're here. All my nurses are virgins."

"Now, I know you is black," replied Old Joe.

In the time he was at the hospital, he had many visits from students and others. One in particular, a cheerleader, told him her private sex life, (giving her boyfriend oral sex in the shower of the mens' locker room while his team mates watched). Then she asked him if he knew other ways to please a man.

He said,"It simple, Baby. Fuck it, suck it, whip it, but don' never bite it off." And he thought to himself, "Why all these young white bitches think Ol' Joe got the pipeline to sex. But on the other hand, I done it every which way 'cept fuckin' on top of a chargin' buffalo."

When he got back to his philosophy class. "Prof" proposed a novel idea.

He said, "Joe, you're really popular with the students. They'd like you to give a two to three hour seminar on any topic that interests you. History, literature, philosophy. The "String theory", whatever. What do you say, Joe?"

"That sound like somethin' interestin'. But where? In the classroom?"

"Wherever you want, Joe," replied the "Prof".

"Why don' I do it down by the river, East River Drive, like Jesus and his Disciples only widout Jesus. They brings they own wine and cheese. They aint be no turnin' water into wine. Ol' Joe aint supernatural. I be gittin' my own P.A. system," said Joe.

"Can I come?" asked the "Prof".

"Sho', wouldn't' have it no other way, Prof."

"Have you something in mind, Joe?" asked the "Prof".

"Sho' do. It go like this. Philosophy, Grim Faerie Tales, and Literature."

On the appointed day, the students were massed by the river, and chanting, "Joe, Joe, Joe." They were drinking large quantities of wine and smoking a particular green substance.

Joe, stood at the P. A. system, and took a giant swig of blackberry brandy from his flask. He cleared his throat and stepped up to the microphone. "Anybody out there who don' know me, I tells ya I be Ol" Joe or Catfish Joe, and it do indeed, look like I be a Fisher of Men, on this here day. And I pray fo' assistance from our Lord today. I wants ya to know I be a plain man widout' no degree or education. But I does a helluva' lot of cogitatin'. We gon' do this the democratic way. Sometimes ya asts me questions and other times I jes' say whut done pop into my head. God help ya. Amen." And Old Joe laughed.

One student asked, "Joe your favorite author?"

"It be an unlikely choice fo' a black man. I always kind of figured crackers was kind of funny. And then I done read Flannery O'Connor's, "A Good Man Is Hard To Find," and find out it true. It really crack me up 'though wid' the plot you might'nt think so. They is a real disgustin' cracker fambly', mom, pops, two kids, and this really fucked up grandmother. Anyway they overturns they car on a back road, and this, crazy psycho, done kill the whole mess of them, the name of Misfit. The grandmother be the main character who done get the fambly' in this fucked up mess. The kid who kill her say, 'She would have been a good woman if it had been somebody to shoot her every day of her life.' And the Misfit, the fucked up psycho, befo' he kill her say, 'there never was a body that give the undertaker a tip.' I don' know bout' you but I thinks this be powerful fuckin' funny. Also, this Flannery be some kind of mean, crazy, white bitch whut I think be real good in bed if she don' bite it off."

There was laughter, and several bravos, and lots of clapping from the students.

"Now, I gon' cover three philosophers, Nietche, Machiavelli, and Sarte."

"Nietche, first.

Generally speakin' the most evil motherfucker whut ever lived! He say there be a kind of man, called the Super Man, who be above all law and morals, and can do anythin' he please cuz he so damn special. Jes' like the Ten Commandments don' exist. It be the exact opposite of Christianity. What if everyone think they be the Super Man? Then the bodies gon' pile up and everyone gon' run the red light. Chillen', fogit' this Nietche shit and git' yo' asses to church. Ya needs The Word."

"Machiavelli, second. Or how to be a Con Man.

This S.O.B. say jes' pretend to be whut you aint to git' over. Ya sees this a lot around election time and if ya don' b'leive me jes' read the paper, or watch the television.

Sartre, third. Existentialism.

He say Life be Absurd and don' mean nothin'. Aint he ever had a piece of tail or drank a glass of wine. This be jes' Bad Attitude. Can't even git no damn ass lookin' like a damned ugly old frog. He got his head up his ass fo' sho'.

"What's next Mr. Joe?" asked a pert blond student who might have been and advertisement for hot chocolate.

"We gon' do Grim Faerie Tales. "

"Goldilocks and the Three Bears."

"The moral of this story is don' fuck wid' anyone whut is bigger than yoself', and if ya does, don' stay round fo' the beat down."

"Lil' Red Riding Hood."

Well, the lil' bitch sho' know how to dress but she aint too swift in the head department. Is you special ed. or high on mushrooms that you aint recognize yo' own granny's face. Futhermo' if yo' grams say she want to "eat" you, ya best book it. Cuz, she a lezzy!"

"Sleeping Beauty."

How ya gon' slay a dragon fo' some bitch you aint never seen? How ya know she aint frigid, ugly, or lezzy? She too high maintenance if ya got to put yo life on the line. They's lots of fine bitches in church or even in bars and ya can see 'em beforehand!".

"Now we gon' switch over to some serious literature. Is ya ready?"

"Edgar Allen Poe."

"I picks him cuz I thinks he be a seriously fucked up white man but he do got talent. I think he like his bitches, beautiful, cold, and dead. I know they be a word fo' this but I aint the most educated man in the world."

"I quotes from his poem, Annabel Lee:

"And so, all the night tide, I lie down by the side,

Of my darling, my darling, my life, and my bride,

In her sepulcher there by the sea,

In her tomb by the sounding sea."

Now I don' know whether this be a white thin' or not but aint no black man ever do this shit. Cuz they aint no fuckin' in the grave! Snap out of it motherfucker!"

Ligeia

In this story, his first wife, Ligeia, be a real stone fox, and she die on him. He take it real bad, and go on the pipe. Then he git' a second wife, Rowena, and she not as fine, and the sucker can't git' no break cuz she die too. He lay her on a slab fo' some reason and I hopes it aint whut you is thinkin'. Then he go back and find the corpse done turned back into his first wife, Ligeia, and she all smilin' and lookin' at him with glittery eyes, and he git' all happy. I don' know 'bout you but this aint make me too happy. I damn sho' book it. 'Nuff said. We moves on.

"My Fair Lady."

First, somethin' wrong wid' this picture. Most mens wants to git' clothes off womins, not put them on womins. Is ya cogitatin"? I think the good professor be gay like that fella', Versace. And 'nother 'thin', this Eliza bitch, aint be too swift. All she know is how to use the right spoon, and dress up. A woman need somethin' in her head. If it be a black bitch she ast him fo' 'bout three credit cards and to put

her ass through college!"

"Wuthering Heights."

"This show that bitches gon' choose the Bling over the cock every time. This bitch, Cathy, grow up wid' a po' gypsy boy, and they falls in love. And then, she go off and marry a gnat dick, rich guy, and leave the po' gypsy boy hangin' high and dry. Then the po' boy go off, git' rich, and come back, and she diein' and astin' to see his ass after she done fuck him over so royally. He mourn her fo' the rest of his life after that horrible fuckin' over. I say, snap out of it, ya dumb bastard. Go out, live, raise a fambly' and don't turn down no ass if it be clean!"

"Lady Chatterly's Lover."

"The husband done got it shot off in the war, and he super rich, so she don' leave him. But her make a mistake of hiring this fine lookin' grounds keeper, name of Mellors. Ya know the bitch gone go for a brother that be packin' every time. The moral of this story is ya best hire a Oriental or Indian gardener, or someone as ugly as mud, and toothless too."

"Now we gone go over to Shakespeare, My Main Man, Hamlet."

"Hamlet got one sonabitchin' problem. His uncle kill his father, the king and marry his mother. This give new meaning to the word, motherfucker. His father come to him as a ghost and demand revenge. He try to handle it but some of his friends say he aint trackin'.

He say, and I quotes:

'I am but mad, north, northwest,

When the wind is southerly,

I know a hawk, from a hand saw.'

This mean I may only be crazy part of the time, or I might not be as crazy as you think. This be the best 'splantion of crazy I ever heard. He kind of do some bad things, like killin' his girl's pops, by accident, and she go plumb crazy. But, remember aint nobody perfect. His girl, Ophelia, be the first abused woman in literature. If it be a black bitch, she aint go crazy. She gone find some way to off him, real slow, and evil."

"Now is everyone of y'al drunk enuff'? I gon' wind up so's ya can all go home and git' some ass or whatever. I hope Ol' Joe aint crippled yo' young minds none. The next thing I got come under the heading of crazy white shit, namely the Marquis de Sade, and The Story of O.

"Marquis de Sade. The World's First Pimp."

This guy like to torture and beat womin's asses so's he can git' it on wid' 'em. He say in his writings, 'I doubt whether any of these bitches feels any pleasure.' How can they when you is beatin' they asses. Plus, I bet my life on it, you wasn't well hung and didn't have no natural rhythm. Or maybe you gay, some kind of way. This aint no black thang, I guarantee. I say if it hurt, I says send it back!"

"The Story of O or the Dumbest Bitch Whut Ever Lived."

This bitch allow her self to be a slave to men, and aint even git' paid fo' her sufferin'. They's some black bitches whut do this kind of thing but it sho' aint free! She wear the back of her skirt cut out and no underwear so's her bare ass touch wherever she sit. And she has to do whoever ast her no questions ast. Bitch aint even git' no weddin' ring, no big house, no Bling! And when she ast her man, Sir Stephen, if she can kill herself, he say "sho' and happy trails." This be some coldass shit. If it be a black bitch she gon' come back and say, "Motherfucker, you aint really love me." Then she gon' blow his motherfuckin' head off wid' a shot gun! Nuff said."

The students stood up and cheered and clasped his hands. One young lady asked him to sign her breasts and he said "Sho', baby, if theys's real.

"Well, youngsters. That's all Ol' Joe got. I hope I aint bored ya none. I gone git' drunk and git' me some poontang, and I hopes ya does the same!"

SLICK

"What is you sayin' boy? Ya wants Ol' Joe to write a book? Does I look like Mark Twain? What yo" name again?" said Joe. Mr. Joe looked at the blond, young, preppy young man, and he thought, "look like a peeled onion wid' arms and legs."

"Sir, I can definitely say not Mark Twain for obvious reasons." He extended a well manicured hand toward Joe which he shook, and said,

"The name's Anthony Shaw, the Third."

"Whatsa matter, they fuck up the first two?" laughed Old Joe.

"Oh, hell yes," replied Anthony.

"I gon' call ya Slick cuz that's whut you is. Is you crazy? Ol' Joe aint got no education or no degree!"

"That's what we want, the working man's perspective on life and literature," replied Slick.

"Son, I aint hardly worked, jes' here and there. Does ya have the right

Joe?"

"Mr. Joe, I went to your seminars down by the river when I was at Penn. You are akin to a Greek Philosopher King."

"A king, definitely not. If I was , I'd have a palace full of pussy. A philosopher, yes but aint everybody? Ya can't help but cogitate. It jes' come natural," replied Joe.

"No, Joe, not everybody's a 'cogitator' as you put it. They rent their empty space to U-Haul."

"Now, I know you is my boy, Slick. How much ya pay me up front?"

"$50,000," replied Slick."Fo' that amount, Ol' joe be willin' to write the book and fuck cows on yo' front lawn," exclaimed Joe.

"Well, so far, so good, Mr. Joe. You are unique," said Slick.

"Eunuch, no I aint, since last time I done looked." And Slick started to reply but Joe stopped him. "Jes' pullin' yo' leg, youngster. That kind of money buy a whole lot of what is good, and some of that which aint. Nothin' devilish, though. Boy, I gon' sign in blood. Would give ya my soul , too, but the Lord done got that."

"That's okay, Mr. Joe. We don't take souls anymore. They crumble like carbon," replied Slick who handed Mr. Joe the contract.

"Boy, you after my own heart. Why aint ya come wid' me to the Top Hat Club fo' some blackberry brandy, and some poontang if ya wants it?"

"Yes, to both," replied Slick.

DOUBLE, DOUBLE, TOIL AND TROUBLE

The girls always met on Friday morning for their coffee klatch. They always met at Myrtle's because her husband was often away on business or so that was his story.

The Devil, a red, horny person also sat in.

By horny, I do not mean in "that" way.

They did not see him nor did they see themselves.

Occasionally, they would smell the scent of burning brimstone.

And one day one of them said,

"What the hell, Myrtle, did you burn the toast?"

And, Myrtle said in jest, "Hell, no, I just singed my cunt hairs from making love with Favio.

"Girl," said Lavinia, "Dorothy Parker's got nothing on you."

"That's the truth," Gladys piped in. "A regular knight of the Algonquin Round Table."

"Come in, girls, before you perish from hunger," said Myrtle.

And they would lumber in the door. Most women glide or slink into a room. The girls lumbered or lurched in like three, amiable Grizzly bears. Between them they weighed eight hundred to one thousand pounds, give or take a ton or two. And they smelled like vanilla cookies and rotten sex.

And before I proceed with my dainty, little tale, I will hasten to describe my three, robust ladies.

Myrtle, the hostess, a peroxide blond wore her hair teased up with a liberal coating of hair spray. To tell the truth, it looked like an insane, little sparrow's nest perched atop her head. She loved the color, Chinese red, and wore it most of the time. It was after a character in a Felini film, Amarcord, named Graciana. When she walked, or undulated, her fat moved in great waves like a great ocean. It was an experiment in liquidity. Her fat all but obscured her sex and this was true of all of them

But, why bother?

All three had long since given up the act of sex. It was but a distant memory like the color, heliotrope. What the hell was it anyway and who the hell cared?

But never mind we will only discuss what really matters.

Most notable thing about Myrtle was her tiny, fat, water logged feet and her extreme fondness for designer shoes, Jimmy Chu, most notably.

Her feet looked like tiny sausages stuffed painfully in their casings.

What one does for Beauty.

Gladys, the most attractive of three, was the kind of woman of which others, would say, "Yes, but what a beautiful face."

She still had the vitality of youth and could move faster than any fat person alive. Her figure was perfectly proportioned like a statue from Gaston Le Chaisse. Her waist was comparatively small and her giant ass looked like two pups fighting in a gunny sack. Black men would follow her down the street, saying lusty remarks

But she would never consider any of them. Not because they were black but because she judged they would never have any money.

A man without money was as useless as a cripple on a bicycle.

She kept herself well for she was vain of porcelain white, lustrous skin, slanted almond eyes, and pouty, red mouth. She only wore bright colors like orange or chartreuse. She said black was for funerals,

And she was far from dead, not by a long shot.

Lavinia, the most educated of the three, had a degree in liberal arts from Sarah Lawrence college. She was fond of quoting poems and literature.

"Mornings, nights, and afternoons, I measure my life with coffee spoons."

And she knew that poem was her life.

So tragic. So true.

When she got out of college, she tried briefly to get a job but they wanted her to type, to be an automaton, a dummy. They just did not recognize intellectual brilliance when they saw it. So she married the first "good provider" when she saw him on the unluckiest day of his life. She thought of him as a white, noxious worm.

A nothing. Of the three, she had the most rage, the most vitriol. She would often spew it out at those closest to her like green, toxic battery acid. She dressed like an earth mother, tapestry or blue jean skirts, peasant blouses, Navaho jewelry, and the ever stylish, Birkenstocks.

A hippie in dress, a bitch in soul.

She was not materialistic like her two girlfriends but she was fat like them resembling a large gourd. A scientific experiment gone terribly, terribly wrong. She felt somewhat superior to the both of them as she had the life of the mind.

Life does indeed sometimes make some strange bed fellows.

One day it struck her to quote Hamlet.

"I am mad, but north, northwest.

When the wind is southerly,

I know a hawk from a handsaw."

"That's Hamlet, the Melancholy Dane.

It's one of the most profound statements in literature.

It's Shakespeare, you know."

She did it to remind her friends that they were illiterate.

"What kind of name's Hamlet," inquired Gladys,

"How about Porkchoplet? And laughed her ass off after a fashion.

Myrtle decided to straighten her out.

"What the fuck, Lavinia that's not real life. And anyway you're not mad, north, northwest, You're crazy all the time, every fucking minute.

Not that there's anything wrong with that."

"You fucking bitch," Lavinia fumed.

Myrtle replied, "Bitch is correct, Babes. And the fucking part is right on, too. I can't get enough of my Henry." And then she laughed like Ethel Merman.

Lavinia. herself laughed, and said,

"To the moon, Alice," and raised her fist in the air.

Then they all laughed.

And one was reminded of the three witches out of MacBeth.

"Double, Double, Toil, and Trouble,

Fire Burn and Cauldron Bubble."

But it could be said that the witches were nicer than our winsome three.

"Oh, girls," said Gladys, "You know how Clive is doing his precious, little anorexic secretary? Well, I pretended I just found out. I tell you Meryl Streep has nothing on me. I cried, I carried on. I said, 'You don't love me any more. Do you want a divorce? You know how much I love you.'"

"And he threw me an expansive bauble to shut me up.

Then it was like Little Miss Muffet had just squashed the spider that sat down beside her. Such a performance, girls. I deserve a medal."

"Tears, Tears, Idle Tears," said Lavinia, ever the literary light.

"Well," said Gladys, spreading out her red, six inch nails in front of her pretty face. "Mama done got some of her own."

The other two girls shrieked and laughed in delight and begged for more details.

"The truth is," said Gladys, "it's the Mexican gardener. He saw me masturbating in front of our picture window one day and the rest is history."

"In front of the window, Gladys," said Lavinia.

"Why the hell not," replied Gladys. "I was all dried up. Heard it might kill ya. And I heard the Latins have rhythm."

"And do they?" inquired Lavinia.

"Nine inches of rhythm and can't get my hand around it," Gladys replied.

Myrtle said, "And what of our club, Sisters Against Cock?"

"Count me out," said Gladys.

"And what, may I ask, do you do for him?" asked Lavinia.

"Anything that's perverted or lewd or both. He licks my, big, white ass like a trained Doberman."

"You're the Whore of Babylon," said Lavinia.

"That's just your opinion, and nobody'd do you. You dried up old cunt."

"Bitch I'm neither too old or fat to kick your natural ass.

Mrytle intervened, "Listen, girls this is unseemly. Ladies discuss, tramps kick ass," Myrtle exspoused.

"Or poison, like our dear friend, Lucretia," said Lavinia.

"Well, at least she was a lady," said Mrytle. Not like that cocksucker, Ted Bundy."

"Girls," said Gladys, "If you're through brutalizing me. A healthy, sensuous, intelligent woman, can we please just move on."

"Oh, what the fuck, Babes" said Mrytle, "We're sorry."

"Ditto," said Lavinia. "Besides why argue with Destiny."

"Oh, now it's Destiny. I thought it was just fucking," said Gladys.

"I just like to give everything a literary turn," said Lavinia.

"All those books have rotted your natural mind," said Mrytle.

Gladys, the softest of the three, said, "Now Myrtle, tell the truth but don't always be telling it. Lavinia didn't mean anything by it. You know how she is. This coffee is a little pale now. Let's break out the brandy."

"At ten in the morning, Gladys?" said Mrytle.

"Hell, yes. Even Jesus drank wine, honey," she replied.

"Well, I guess you're right, Gladys,

"None of us are on the old nine to five," said Myrtle who launched into an entirely different direction.

"Anybody want cake? I got coconut or chocolate mousse."

"I'll have a little of both. I wouldn't want to be a segregationist," intoned Lavinia.

"Good one, Lavinia, now I got one." She held up a can of V-8, and said, "Anathema. Didn't know I knew such big words, did you, Bitch? On another topic entirely, how's old gnat dick doing, Lavinia?"

"Puny as ever," Lavinia replied. "Tries to rub that pathetic, little thing on my leg and I tell him I'm going to kick his ass."

"God, you're rough, Lavinia," said Gladys. "I only say I have clamidia, or some other STD. Never, AIDS because that just wouldn't be funny."

"We don't want to be cruel, girls," interjected Myrtle.

"Right, we're just assertive, that's all," piped Lavinia.

"Honey," said Myrtle, "I believe you're a bit more than just assertive."

Lavinia replied, "Who cares. I give him all this shit and he just loves me all the more. Some men just like shit. What can I say."

"Well spoken, Marquessa de Sade. See, I do read certain things"said Gladys.

"I'm impressed, Gladys. I thought you only read Jackie Collins or Barbara Cartland," said Lavinia.

"Now, wait just a goddamed minute," interjected Myrtle. "I think Jackie Collins is a fine writer. I have all her books. She can really spin a plot. It sure keeps me on edge."

"That's because you ain't had no dick in twenty years," said Gladys.

"Shut up, Gladys or shall I say Lady Chatterly? It's not that we can't.

We just choose not to. Makes you sweat and the smell is God awful. Though sometimes though I get in moods where I just have to have it," said Myrtle.

"And I get out of breath and get cramps in my ass," Lavinia added.

Well, that's certainly reason enough," said Gladys diplomatically.

Never speak too much of one's good fortune. The jackals might come in the night and take it all away. This thought wafted through her brain like wisps of smoke from a campfire.

"Oh, girls," said Lavinia. "I've got exciting news. I'm writing a novel, and surprise, it's a romance novel."

"And we thought you hated that kind of writing," said Myrtle.

"It's all in how it's done. I think I know enough about love to write a real page turner," said Lavinia.

The room went silent, eyebrows were raised and looks exchanged.

And the Devil laughed but they didn't hear him.

"What might I ask is the plot?" queried Myrtle.

"Well it's kind of like an O'Henry plot twist," replied Lavinia.

"I see,"said Mrytle, but she didn't.

"Tell us more, dear," said Gladys.

"Well, it's about a married woman, middle aged whose husband doesn't appreciate her," replied the future author.

"Pure Jackie Collins, so far," said Myrtle. "And does she find true love with a really hot man and move to a charming cottage by the sea?"

"No, Myrtle," said future genius, "This is a woman of character, educated, well read, creative, and refined and she's being stifled by an empty, meaningless life. Oh, yes, and passion simmers just below the surface but this is not readily apparent. This woman is not a whore."

"Oh, yeah," said Gladys.

"Anyway," said genius, "She turns to this gorgeous gay man, a talented, successful portrait painter for solace and comfort in her lonely, desolate life. It's innocent enough in the beginning. But I need to tell you that she's extremely attractive in an earthy way. Kind of like a young Sophia Loren. Then one day as he is painting her nude, kind of like the portrait of the Duchess of Alba, but you wouldn't know this. Anyway for the first time in his life he becomes madly, insanely aroused by her vibrant womanhood. And he rips off his clothes and brutally rapes her. And she comes for the first time in her life. It's like the opening of a really ripe, beautiful orchid, you see. He even gets cerulean blue in her cunt. But never mind, that's just poetic license. They run off together and get married, and he forswears men forever."

"And they live happily ever after," said Myrtle dryly. "No Jackie Collins heroine ever fucked a queer. That's for damn sure."

Lavinia further explained, "She's just the quintessential woman, waiting to be discovered and made whole by true passion. A complex character. A powerful woman.

Myrtle replied, "Yes, I can see that, Lavinia."

"Bravo," said Gladys, "Send me the first copy."

Then Lavinia suddenly stood up and looked at her watch.

"Oh shit," she exclaimed. "It's nearly three and I'm blasted. I've got to pick up the rug rat, or more poetically, the fruit of my loins. The things I do for that little bastard. I can't wait until he goes off to boarding school."

"Well, Lavinia, dear, remember us when you get rich and famous,"

said Mrytle.

"Sorry we don't have a bottle of champagne to break over a ship or something," said Gladys.

"You Bitches are the greatest," said Lavinia.

And they all parted as friends for what else would they do. After she left there was a silence like the Great Arctic North.

Then Gladys said soflly, "Well, Myrtle, what do you really think?"

Myrtle replied, "Total shit. I wouldn't wipe my ass with it."

And they both laughed like the wild hyenas on the Serengeti. The Devil, in the mean time, had been listening to everything. He put the tip of one finger in his mouth, then drew an invisible, vertical line in the air, in a gesture that could only mean "Score one for me." Then he wrote three words in his notebook, DEFINITELY PRIME MEAT.

THE BATTLE OF THE LESSENING PULCHRITUDE

The girls were meeting again at Myrtle's and this time they were going to skip the cake and go directly to the booze. A liquid diet, so to speak. Lavinia liked things not too sweet or frothy, drinks indicative of her class and education. Myrtle and Gladys liked anything with whipped cream and miniature umbrellas that required a blender. They liked things that went fizz in the night. As Myrtle, would often say if it was not sweet it tasted like semen.

They were, on this day, all arrayed in their Tommy Hilfinger sweats looking like a basketball team gone to ruin or a field gone to fallow.

"We really should exercise more, girls. The most exercise I get is when I swipe my husband's credit cards. You know I hate that bitch Susan Lucci looking al swelte and being old as God! Damnation!"

Gladys laughed, and said, "Myrtle, you are a piece of work,"

"As are you dearie," she replied.

"And what about me?" inquired Lavinia.

"You're Satan's whore. He's the only man brave enough to fuck you!"

"No, I think it'd be a little on the cold side. On the serious side, Albert got tough. Said he'd divorce me is I didn't screw him."

"Well that's something. Old gnat dick grew some balls," mused Gladys.

"Always had them. They were just neglected, poor things," remarked Myrtle.

"Shall I hit you again, Gladys. You're low on the drinkie poo."

"Sure, Babe, Sobriety is the bane of my existence."

"I'll have another glass of Chardonnay. Get rid of this fucking little wine glass and give me a water glass so you don't have to keep jumping up and down," interjected Lavinia.

"So, Lavinia, what are you doing for old Al?" asked Myrtle.

"I sit on this face. That way I don't have to do anything."

"And nothing else?"

"I get the microscope and jerk him off," replied Lavinia.

"Oh, really," said Gladys archly. "I know that wouldn't satisfy my Enrique. He likes a little lip action."

Well, he thought so too. So, how can I say this. I might, I just might have bit him just the slightest bit."

"Damn," exclaimed Myrtle, "are you a fucking piranha, Lavinia?"

"Most assuredly so," she replied.

"Did he pop you one?" inquired Gladys.

"He came like Krakatoa and then lay in my arm crying like a baby afterward. Now I only do it on special occasions like when he brings me a bauble. He loves the shit out of me."

"We love you, too. Fortunately we're not lesbians. You'd probably bite off our tits," said Myrtle.

"No, I wouldn't. You guys must think I'm horrible."

"It's why we like you, Babes," she replied, "Next to you, Gladys and I are like pristine little angel pussy playing harps on some cloud."

"I resent that, Myrtle, I always give to the homeless and I never ask them what they're going to do with the money. Hell, if I were on the street, I'd want to be stoned, too."

"You're not even on the street and you want to be stoned," said Gladys.

"All great artists suffer, Gladys. They seek solace in drink and other things. Look at Poe. He was a drunk and a dope fiend."

"I see," said Gladys, shooting a microscopic glance at Myrtle who winked.

"Well, darling," she further inquired, "How's the writing coming?"

"I've made a detailed outline. You know, beginning, middle and end."

"What else have you done with it?" interjected Myrtle.

"Well, I've got a rhyming dictionary for the love talk."

"To rhyme what, love? Luck and fuck," quipped Gladys.

"You guys put me down all the time. Just because I'm trying to do something with my life besides conspicuous spending," said Lavinia.

"True, Babes. We never knew a writer before. We just don't understand your process," said Myrtle.

"It's nothing you'd understand. I'm filling the pond."

"And would that be Walden Pond, dearie?" said Gladys.

"You sarcastic, bitch, Gladys. You've never read that. You probably just saw the title somewhere!" said Lavinia.

"Sugar plum, I have on occasion cracked a book while I'm frying bacon or ironing. You know sometimes I even find I like Emily Dickinson. The Russians that Clive tries to get me to read just give me a headache. Doestoevsky is a toilet book in my house."

"I'm impressed, Gladdy. Myrtle you should try to improve you mind too."

"I'm rich, honey. I don't need a mind." Myrtle replied.

"Fucking A. That way if you lost it, you'd never know," said Lavinia who roared with laughter.

"Seriously, Lavinia, you should be farther along," said Myrtle. "Do at least two chapters a day. Set yourself a schedual."

"What the fuck you think I am, Myrtle. The Little Train That Could?"

"No, indeed, my girl, you are not that. You're more like Tillie the Hun."

"You always know how to make me laugh Myrt. How's the little snot nose doing. Still making A's and going to plays?"

"First, do not, I repeat, do not, call my little Conchita a snot nose or I'll tear you a new one!"

"Sorry, sweetie, I know you love her loads. And why not she looks like a little movie star."

"Apology accepted. She's only nine and first in her class, and she plays Mozart like it was he, himself, hitting the keys. She'll never have to dirty her ass for any man."

"Bravo," said Lavinia, and Gladys did too.

"Myrt," asked Gladys, "Why'd you name her Conchita. Neither you nor Henry are Spanish."

"But the upstairs maid was when Henry was balling her on my bed and I was pregnant. That little rotten toothed, knock kneed bitch. I sent her packing. Told her if she wanted to stay she'd have to do me too. Boy, was I hot. So, I named her Conchita after the maid just to remind Henry not to take himself too seriously again in our house."

"And do you think he's faithful to you now," asked Lavinia.

"Oh, hell, no. But I don't care as long as it's not right under my nose. I love the hell out of that handsome fucker."

"But don't you think he's fucking you over?" said Lavinia.

"Any time he wants and anywhere," replied Myrtle.

"I still think you should stand up to him," persisted Lavinia.

Why when I can lie down for him?" said Myrtle who blasted the room with her laughter.

"Myrtle, you're a helluva woman even if you've only read the funnies," said Lavinia.

"Can't. They're too deep for me, Babes!"

"You know, girls, this is on a completely different topic. I've been feeling something is missing from our lives lately. I think we need spiritual enlightenment," said Gladys.

"As in God?" queried Lavinia.

"Yes, as in God," she replied. "We're too secular. Ass deep in diamonds, mink stoles, limos, and caviar. What about the true meaning in life?"

"Satre said that life is absurd, meaningless. It's called existentialism," said Lavinia.

"I'd call it a crock of shit," replied Myrtle. "I have too much fun to believe that crap. Do, you believe that Lavinia?"

Well, no. I find meaning in my art,"

"Oh, give it a break, Lavinia. You've got children, a husband who worships you and us, your dear friends. Life is about a lot more than art!" said Myrtle.

"Girls, our souls are in mortal danger and we must act before it's too late!" said Gladys.

"That's because you're up to your ass in semen and it's not even Clive's," snapped Lavinia.

"Lavinia, shut the fuck up!" snapped Myrtle. "Never talk to our Gladdie that way, and I'm going to throw the Bible at you now. Judge Not Lest Ye Be Judged. If Gladdie says we're going to church, we're going to goddamned church!"

"I'm sorry, I know I'm too caustic sometimes. Mother used to call me Little Poisonous Olive Oyl."

"Now, Gladdie, what church?" asked Myrtle.

"I don't know. We're all Protestants. What's the difference."

"Let's let our fingers do the walking through the Yellow Pages. You're it, Gladdie, You choose. Just close your eyes and do it,"

"Oh, just like Russian roulette," quipped Lavinia.

"Exactly, so," said Myrtle drily.

Her finger selected Mount Zion Baptist Church.

"Oh hell, no Myrt," said Lavinia. "That's a black church. Not that there's anything wrong with it. Select again, Gladys."

"I won't choose again. God guided my hand," replied Gladys.

"Did God also guide mine," asked Lavinia showing her the middle finger.

"No, love," replied Myrtle. "I suspect it was the Other Fellow who guided your hand."

GOD IN HER PANTS

They went to Mount Zion Baptist Church the following Sunday and they were late, but not disastrously so. They were pearls in a sea of obsidian, and if not pearls, they were certainly round. They were late because they had to remake Lavinia in her peasant blouse, tapestry skirt, and ever present Birkenstocks. They were not pleased with her new hairdo, a pile of African braids.

"What the fuck's with the hairdo? Did you think you could pass? Jeez, and the giant hoop ear rings?" asked Myrtle.

"You know, when in Rome…" replied Lavinia.

"You cannot wear these clothes, Lavinia," reproached Myrtle. "It's not the sixties.

Do you want to remind them we killed Martin Luther King?".

"I did no such thing. I was at a Crisco party at the time. You know, Free Love," replied Lavinia.

"Was that before you knew you could charge," said Gladys archly.

"Bitch!" replied Lavinia.

"Seriously, dear, show some respect. Here, put on this red Calvin suit with a Vera blouse, and get out of those hideous Jesus shoes!" said Myrtle.

"I think I look just fine."

"Well, you don't. And put on some base, lipstick, and eye shadow."

"I'm naturally pretty. I don't need all that shit! Next thing I know you'll want me to put on some of those hideous heels."

"No, to the first, yes to the second. You look like Abbie Hoffman's woman!" said Myrtle.

"This is character assassination!"

"No, dear, it's fashion assassination!" replied Myrtle.

"I feel like I'm betraying my true self."

"It gets easier the more you do it," replied Myrtle.

The black people welcomed them at the door with clasps of hands and kisses on the cheeks. One robust lady all decked out in a hot pink suit hugged Lavinia, and said, "Girl, you look fine on this day of our Lord." Lavinia noted the scent of baby powder emanating from the woman, and also the radiance of good shining in her sweet face, and thought, "I must use this in my novel." The elder deacons were also at the door welcoming people in. They were still, good men in muted suits of black, brown and green. As people get older character gets etched into their features. Good radiates: evil implodes.

Al three felt the power of faith as a solid, palpable presence like a stone in the mist. The colors of red, navy, chartreuse, orange, and pink gleamed throughout the congregation, and the black ladies had on their Sunday hats. Sly hats gliding over foreheads in waves, happy hats resting like bird's nests on bowed heads, and prim hats of straw with navy ribbons. Many of the ladies wore short white gloves, and their hands in unison fanned their warm, honeyed faces in the still, summer air. The men, more sedate in muted colors, sat quietly composed.

The little girls looked like lace doilies in their organza, silk or cotton party dresses. The young boys wore their suits proudly, hoping to slide into powerful Godly manhood like their fathers.

They listened to the music and were transported from their lives of privilege and materialism. The men's choir sang, "Our God Is An Awesome God" in voices of tenor, and bass. Gladys leaned over to Myrtle, saying, "All that testosterone from Our Lord."

Myrtle replied crisply, "You are inappropriate, my girl."

Gladys only flashed her a seamless smile. Then they all shook in the presence of "The Voice." It came from a little, old, black woman dressed in a cheap red and white dress and straw hat. Her skin, blue black, was stretched tightly over sharp, chisled features. The voice didn't so much as come from her mouth: it burst forth from her chest like a wound. It exploded from her soul, deep, powerful, and raspy. She sang, "That

Old Rugged Cross". The congregation swayed, and fans fluttered like dove wings in the air.

There was a hushed silence in the room as the pastor ascended the pulphit. He was a panther of a man, lean and full of sinew. He had the face of an Ethiopian prince. He spoke and gave thanks to Sister Elmira for her singing, and the congregation stood up and applauded. She bent her head in humble thanks. There were some loud "amens" and "praise Jesuses". Then he waved one still hand across the air and everyone sat down, and became silent.

"Who amongst us has not sinned," he intoned in a baritone voice. Myrtle restrained Lavinia from raising her hand.

"It's a rhetorical question, Lavinia, and besides you're a bitch, and that's a sin."

"I am not,"

"Please," said Myrtle rolling her eyes.

Gladys turned to them with a fierce frown and they fell silent.

"My sermon today is on the sanctity of marriage. The Holy Covenant between man and wife." Gladys dropped her fan and Lavinia flashed her an evil grin, piranha to minnow.

"Who amongst us has not strayed even if only in mind? If you have lusted in your heart only, it is the same in the eyes of the Lord, as doing the act. The love a man has for his wife is sacred: the love of a wife for her husband is sacred. Matrimony is a Holy state. Can I get an amen?"

Gladys felt a flutter in her heart and lower down. "He's so good," she thought, and "so manly."

Myrtle watched her and saw a change in focus.

"Gladdy, you best not think what you're thinking. We're in a church."

"Do you read minds?"

"No, but I can hear radios, and yours is one. Besides, you're flushed, and sweating like you've just run a marathon. Cool off before you become a goddamned orchid,"

"Ladies, how many times have you lusted in your hearts or denied your man's desires?" said the pastor.

Gladys felt like he was talking directly to her. She pressed her legs together and felt a jolt of lightening down below, and thought, "This can't be from God. But, on the other hand, he did create twats. God in my pants."

"Enough," said Myrtle, pinching her arm. "You're like a cat in heat."

"What are you two whispering about?" inquired Lavinia.

"Nothing," replied Myrtle. "I'm just sick of all the goddamn sinning going on in this world!"

Then the minister went into several Biblical instances of malfeasance and the penalties for adultery. He closed with a graffic description of Hell, and a sincere call for universal marital fidelity.

"God! I can smell the devil's balls sizzling on brimstone," intoned Lavinia. Myrtle and Gladys shot her horrified glances, and Gladys made the "shush" gesture, finger to lip.

Myrtle said to her friends, "I'm going to try to be a better person from now on, and not be such a bitch. Quit drinking so much, and wanting to kick model ass. And also quit bankrupting my Henry."

"That'll work for you," said Lavinia.

"Then you're not going to change, Lavinia?"

"Matter cannot be created nor destroyed," she replied.

"Sure it can. How do you explain babies, or cultured pearls, for that matter?"

"Nah. It will always be plain old table salt, and the same for me. I'm just what I am," replied Lavinia.

Gladys shushed them again, and whispered, "I will run over you with my car!"

They remained quiet for the remainder of the time out of respect for the congregation. They hoped their whispers were not heard by anyone human, or anyone else.

There was a cold spot in the church where no one sat. And no one saw the invisible smile on a wickedly handsome face.

THE DEVIL MADE HER DO IT

Myrtle was hosting a girl scout meeting for her daughter, Conchita, the following Wednesday after their sojourn to the church, and Lavinia was assisting. Ordinarily, it would have been Gladys because Myrtle didn't like the idea of leaving Lavinia alone with the children.

Gladys had begged off saying she had some landscaping to do. Upon hearing this, Lavinia had quipped, "I bet she's got a big bush on the land that needs attending".

Myrtle had chortled, and said, "Bitch".

"You know it and proud to be one," replied Lavinia. Myrtle had baked three trays of brownies, one pecan, and had made an orange cake from scratch.

"I don't know why you just didn't use Dunkin Hines, Mrs. Cleaver," interjected Lavinia.

"You wouldn't understand since your idea of mothering is to feed your children live snakes!"

"Ouch! You're abusing the help," said Lavinia.

"So, I am," replied Myrtle as she handed her plates of honey encrusted peanuts, Hersey's kisses, and popcorn to be placed on her pristine, glass end tables. She had stocked the refrigerator with various juices, whole milk, and had made a rather dramatic punch, dollops of lime sherbet floating in Mountain Dew. It rather looked like an atomic melt down or three mile island. Dainty lace encrusted paper cups surrounded the crystal punch bowl.

Lavinia brought a bottle of Abolut for the "big kids" as she put it, or "brat remedy." Myrtle immediately regretted asking for her help.

"Damn bitch is like an alligator mother, apt to eat her young," she mused. Lavinia was a vision in leopard tights, a white peasant blouse, a wooden beaded necklace and ear rings to match, and the ever present Birkenstocks. Myrtle, attired in pink lace, looked like a giant bowl of strawberry ice cream, quivering. As they ambled about the living room placing things here and there, the floor boards creaked, and the cat hid under the couch as if expecting an earthquake. Shortly, the door bell began to ring and the little girls began to trickle in in two's and three's like soft pretty butterflies. There were two little, red haired, brown eyed twins named Sunny, and Sammy, who bought a bouquet of daisies which Myrtle made much of, brushing the tops of their heads with lush, pink kisses. Lavinia leaned into Myrtle's ear and hissed, "wilted". Myrtle ignored this, and continued greeting the girls. They were mostly brunettes with earnest brown eyes and cute pink smiles, little paper dollies all cut from the same chain. One blond child stood out from all the others much as a diamond would stand out in a sea of pebbles. Her bright indigo eyes slanted in a seductive line across her flawless porcelain face and her wild, pouty lips belonged not to any nine year old in this world. Her budding breasts and widening hips proclaimed early womanhood. She held a white teddy bear clutched tightly to her chest, and in her eyes was a look of fearful anticipation.

"And what's your name, honey," asked Myrtle.

"Cecilia," replied the child, her cheeks dimpling like a valentine cupid.

"That's a mighty cute bear you have, honey, and what's his name?"

"Freddie, and he's my bestest friend."

"Your scout uniform's a bit tight in places, baby. Would you like me to give your mommy the name of a tailor?"

"Mommy says' I'm getting too grown up for my age," replied the child.

"Like in what way?" asked Myrtle.

"Sometimes, I do weird things I shouldn't do."

"What kinds of things, sweetheart?"

The child teared up and ducked her head saying nothing.

"You don't have to tell this nosy old woman anything, honey. Besides some people say I'm weird too, and you can see I'm okay, can't you? Now go on in and get yourself some punch. See your friends."

The girl teared up again, and said, "They don't like me any more. Sunny and Sammy say the boys like me now 'cause I'm getting boobies."

"Now that's not very nice," replied Myrtle. "They're just jealous. Don't let those mean girls hurt your feelings."

"They make me feel real sad."

"It's okay to feel sad sometimes, honey, because it always goes away. And between you and me, you're the prettiest little girl here, and the nicest."

"I am?" she said brightening.

"Cross my heart," said Myrtle who placed her hand gently on top of Cecilia's head as she headed for the living room.

"Damn little bitches," she thought, and then. "Conchita better not be in on this shit!"

As Myrtle went in the dining room she was astounded to see that Lavinia was serving up the punch with one hand and taking swigs of Absolut from the bottle with the other. Her wedding ring glistened like Artic ice in the afternoon sun, and the lace curtains made little patterns of light and shade on her skin giving it a mottled, reptilian look. Life imitating art was the thought that popped into her mind.

Lavinia was asking each girls name, and making up absurd rhymes for each girl's name. For Myrtle's own daughter, she made up this rhyme,

"It couldn't be neata'
To be with Conchita.
Hope the bears don't eat her."

She was further giving her own interpretation of well known fairy tales.

"You know, girls, Goldilocks just wasn't to swift to eat up all the bears' food and stick around for them to kick her ass. And Miss Muffit, girls, really! Just what is a tuffit? Can you get them at IKEA, and how do you sit on them. As for the spider, that's right on, girls. Run if you see spiders. And as for Babar, the Elephant, gay as a two dollar bill. I kid you not!"

At this point, Myrtle intervened. "Girls, Miss Lavinia's a little under the weather, and may have head problems. Don't listen to her. Come to the living room and we'll recite the pledge, and sit in a nice circle on the floor."

To Lavinia, she hissed, "Get your ass out of here and go home!"

"Not a chance," replied Lavinia. "And miss the nature talk?"

When they got settled, Sammy, one of the twins raised her hand

and asked Myrtle what "gay" was.

"It's exceptionally happy, baby," replied Myrtle. "Now, let's all hold hands as we say the pledge. It means you really mean it."

"And if we don't?" interjected, Sunny, the other twin."

"You're too young not to mean it!" replied Myrtle. "Now, girls, why is it important to be helpful, trusty and brave?"

A little brunette girl raised her hand, and replied, "Because it's nice, and the right thing to do."

"Bravo! And you get a prize. Lavinia, give me the little giraffe from the big box."

She handed the toy to Myrtle, saying under her breath, "I never got jack shit for any of that." Myrtle shushed her and gave the room her most radiant smile.

"Now, girls, if your brother or sister makes you really, really mad, what do you do?"

"Try to reason with them," replied the same mousy little girl.

"That's not what I do," interjected Sammy. "Knock their block off if they're littler and go to mommy if they're bigger than me."

Before Myrtle could reply, Lavinia was at the box and handing a soft, pink bear to Sammy, saying, "And you get the prize!"

"But I want the prize!" said the other girl in a loud voice. "Mines was the best answer!"

"You're right, too, honey," replied Myrtle, "So right you get the Barbie Doll. Girls, as I said, Miss Lavinia's not herself today. Ignore her."

"I'm always myself," replied Lavinia.

"And so was Lucretia Borgia," snapped Myrtle. "Why don't you just take that bottle and go home!"

"What and miss the nature lesson. Listen up, girls, Miss Myrtle doesn't know anything about nature so I'm going to lead this talk. Girls, what do you do to start a fire when you're all alone in the woods?".

Another child replied. "You just rub two sticks together until they catch fire."

"You could do that, sure. But it would take a long, long time. But on the other hand, don't go to the woods if you're stupid. Bring matches!"

"What if it was in prehistoric times?" said the same child.

"Can you see that happening, baby. What's past is past. If it were prehistoric times, a saber toothed tiger would probably eat you before you could make any kind of fire! Now what do you do if you see a bear around your campsite?"

Cecilia raised her hand. "You've got the floor, young lady," said Lavinia.

"First of all, don't make them mad. Don't excite them. Don't run 'cause they're faster, and let them have all the food."

"Very very good, young lady. But this goes back to stupid. Never ever go to the woods without a gun!"

"Lavinia, that's just about enough of your smart Alec attitude. Girls let's talk abou tour most favorite things in the world. Mine is my husband, Henry, and chocolate cake."

The little wan, mousy girl answered first. Her hair straggled down her back like strands of wet seaweed and she picked at her nails as she talked.

"I like it when mommy hugs me after baking bread. It smells all sweet and like a happy, happy thing. And she always gives me a piece of raw dough 'cause I like it the best and she always tells daddy I made the bread."

There were a few giggles and nudges at this confession. Then Sunny shared next. "I guess I like Christmas best because you get lots of stuff and there's always lots to eat and the grownups always get drunk and say funny things about each other. Sometimes they even fight."

Her twin replied that she liked Halloween the best because she always got to be a black cat, "the most beautiful thing in the world".

"I'd rather be a puppy dog," replied Cindy, a thin wisp of a girl, fragile as a fall leaf. "They're friendlier. For me, the best thing is my ballet class. I know all the positions and how to leap real real high, and teacher says I may be famous one day. I think it's better to have lots of people love you than just one. Because the one could leave and, you know, break your heart."

Lavinia said, "Wisdom at such a young age." And Myrtle said, "Shut up, Lavinia and make yourself a salami sandwich and sober up. These are girls scouts not harlots!"

"What's a harlot?" asked Sunny.

"Some very good, good people are harlots and some very bad people are harlots honey. Don't worry about it until you get older," replied Myrtle.

"Is a harlot a bad woman like a whore?" asked the meek girl.

"Don't go there, sweet girl. Girl scouts are rarely whores. Do you even know what one is?"

"Aunt Cynthia is one. Mommy says so."

"Do you know what it means, honey?" asked Myrtle.

"It means a bad woman. That's all I know," replied the girl.

"Bad is like robbing banks or shooting someone. Only grownups can be bad not little girls. You don't worry about this anymore, little miss, okay? Lavinia, go see where Cecilia is. I think she got lost. This is a big old house."

Imagine Lavinia's surprise when upon opening the door to Myrtle's bed room she saw little Cecilia spread eagled on her plush, four postered, red velvet bed masturbating with the end of her ornate, silver hairbrush.

Lavinia's mouth flew open and she rapidly and quietly shut the bed room door. Cecelia sat up abruptly, pulling down her skirt. Her eyes filled up with tears and her pretty face imploded upon itself. She began to sob.

"Please don't tell mommy, Miss Lavinia. I know I'm bad but I just couldn't help it. It got so hot and burny down there. I know something's really wrong with me."

Lavinia took the little girl in her arms and said, "Nobody's telling anybody anything. Not even Myrtle. What does your mommy say about this?"

"She says it's the devil, and I'm never going to heaven." Then she shook with convulsive sobs.

"Well, I don't want to dispute your mommy, honey, but lots of women get that burny sensation down there and they don't go to hell. It's just that you're a bit young to be having these feelings. Have you bled down there yet?"

"Uh huh," replied Cecelia.

"Have you ever kissed any boys yet?"

"No, but I think about it."

"Uh huh," said Lavinia who kept silent for a few minutes. "Honey, what religion are your parents?"

"Born again Christians."

"Oh shit," replied Lavinia.

"You said a bad word, Miss Lavinia. You're going to hell, too."

"Granted, honey. But we got a problem, here."

"Are you of the devil, Miss Lavinia? If you are I have to run."

"No, I am not, sweetie. I'd just like to help you in some way."

"Do, I need help, Miss Lavinia?"

"Yes, darling, you do. Do you have brothers and sisters, baby?"

"One of each. Why?"

"I suspect your mommy has that burny sensation there too, baby, or you wouldn't have brothers and sisters, and you wouldn't have even been born."

"No, that can't be. Mommy's on God's team, and children come from God. Mommy says so."

"Honey, that feeling makes women do things with men and then they get babies. It was God, not the devil, who made us this way. We're all the same."

"Impossible. Mommy would never be bad."

"Listen, baby, can you trust old Lavinia a tiny, teensy bit?

"Yes, I guess so."

"Then give me your full name, address, and phone number because I have to talk to your parents."

"You're going to tell on me and you said you wouldn't," said Cecilia who began to sob again.

"No, baby, I won't tell. That hasn't changed. You see when girls become woman they get feelings down there. Remember when you were young and you first jumped into a swimming pool? Remember how it was, so cool and tingly? Well, this isn't any different. If God didn't make us this way we wouldn't be this way. It's natural. It isn't the devil like your mommy says. She's confused. Grownups make mistakes too. I just want to talk to her a little bit. So give me your information, sweetie, okay?"

The child gave her what she wanted and they both went downstairs.

Myrtle asked why we were gone so long and Lavinia replied that they were so mesmerized by the fish tank they lost track of time. Myrtle evinced the thought that Lavinia was teaching her the "black arts".

Lavinia replied, "No, dear, she already knows them."

A VISIT FROM SATAN

On Saturday Lavinia stood before Cecilia's house her hand frozen in air.

"Should I ring the door bell or pound on the door like the wrath of Jehovah innie menie minie mo?" she thought. She went with the pounding.

Cecilia answered the door and her eyes popped open like two startled party balloons, and she said, "Miss Lavinia, I didn't know it was you. Mommy thought it was the Jehovah's Witnesses and to tell them we were Buddhists and to go away."

"Isn't lying against God's rules, baby?"

"Mommy says it isn't lying. It's only joking and that God understands."

"I'll just bet he does, honey. Cecilia, let me in. I have to talk to your parents, and no, I won't tell. I promise, baby. And promises fly up to heaven and they're with God, and can't be broken."

"You swear?"

"I swear on my life, sweetie pie. Now go get your parents."

Daddy's on a retreat, and mommy hasn't got up yet."

"Get her up, babes. I've got things on my mind."

Cecilia went upstairs to get her mom up, and Lavinia had the opportunity to appraise the living room. She saw ranch furniture, ceramic cats and elves, a worn, woven braid rug and numerous signs on the wall like, "God Bless Our Happy Home," and "The Lord Giveth And The Lord Taketh." Nowhere did she see a book shelf, only several well used Bibles laying on the old wooden side tables. Prominently displayed in the dining room was a drug store Jesus with blue sequined eyes, and arms outstretched. A yellow circle was behind his head in semblance of a halo. It was a very large portrait, maybe three by five.

"And I thought Jesus had brown eyes. Maybe the Aryan Nation was right after all," she mused.

Cecilia's mother came down yawning, with tousled blond hair, clothed in an old white bath robe that was frayed at the sleeves. But it was her eyes that alarmed Lavinia, blue, empty, dazed, not of this world.

"Shit, she looks like one of those Manson bitches," she thought. "Hi, I'm Lavinia Hanson, a counselor at Cecilia's school, and I've come to talk to you about your young daughter."

"Has she done anything wrong? Is it about boys?" queried the mother.

"What is your first name, please?"

"Florence," replied the woman, her mouth forming into a tight yellow line. "Is it boys?", she inquired again.

"No, Florence, she's done nothing wrong. It's simply that she's becoming a young woman, and we're wondering if she's receiving an adequate sex education at home."

"Do not use that filthy word in my house. It's ungodly," countered Florence.

"Excuse me," said Lavinia who drew an invisible horizontal line in the air with her sharp, sculpted fingernail. "I suggest, Florence, that we send your daughter upstairs while we have a little woman to woman talk. Can we agree to that, Florence? I suggest strongly that you agree to this, dear." Lavinia drew herself up to the full five feet nine and stared down at Florence. Lavinia had a way of looking like one of the Furies, or an avenging angel at the very least.

"Go upstairs, Ceci, mommy is busy."

Cecilia looked from one adult to the next in extreme dismay. She was not used to seeing adults in conflict. Mostly they just said things like, "God is good," or "Praise Jesus." She went up the stairs with a quivering in her heart, and a weakness in her knees. Was this like when David slew Goliath she wondered.

Listen, bitch," hissed Lavinia, "sex is not dirty and it was God who made twats, yours included, which I might add you've obviously been using. I'm not for preteen sex but I am for taking precaution just in case. Nature may take its course a little sooner than planned if you receive my meaning."

"You can't talk to me in my own house like this!"

"I can and will. You're about to ruin your lovely, little daughter. I can talk to you any way I goddamn please!"

"You're crazy! I'll call the police! I'll call your school and get your fired!"

"My school? Listen, cunt, I'm not from any school, and my husband's richer than yours will ever be. You pick up that phone and I'll rip it off the wall and stuff it up your ass. You're going to listen to me!"

"You're Satan. You're the force of evil. I'll get out my cross and vanquish you to the hell you came from!"

"Oh, please, bitch. I'm not a vampire and that cross is just a piece of jewelry. Here is a xanax. Take it, you need it. But what you really need is xyprexa!"

"It's poison! I won't take it!" screamed Florence.

"Then what the hell. Take a shot." And Lavinia handed her her silver flask of brandy.

"You can go to jail for this harassment," replied Florence.

"If I did I'd fuck the warden, get out, and come kill your ass!" laughed Lavinia. "Now Listen, Florence, you will stop these hysterics right this minute while I talk sense to you. Here take a swig. God'll understand. I am not a poisoner."

Florence looked sheepish and timidly reached out for the flask taking a virginal slug.

"Your little girl is extremely sexual and mature for her age. Scolding her, punishing her, and telling her that born again devil shit is not going to work. It didn't work on you either, did it? Get real, honey. Besides it's natural and normal. It is not, I repeat, not, the devil. I could try child abuse because that's what it is but some fucked up, right wing, Republican judge would just let you off because you're Christian. No, I've got a whole 'nother plan for you."

"You can't do anything to us. We walk in God's light. We know what is right. We can raise our children anyway we choose. This is America!" asserted Florence.

"I expected this from you, lady, but I am never ever defeated. Comprende? When does your husband get home?"

"Tomorrow but he won't listen to your Satanic harangue either!"

"No, of course, he wouldn't listen to me. But he will listen to my fricnd.

He's an old Italian man, very old world if you receive my meaning.

And he'll have some cute pink pills for your little girl to take every twenty eight days. And he's so not a gentleman. Absolutely no table manners. And we'll hook up your other girl child, too, when her time comes. Do we understand ourselves now, Florence?"

"You're going to have the mafia force us? You're crazy. Absolutely crazy!"

"That I am but so are you, dearie. As for mafia, there's no such thing. He's just a concerned citizen," said Lavinia who ran her long fingernail down Florence's forearm.

"Oh, yes, and I'm leaving this xanax for you. Take it. You really need it. I'll be back to check on your precious, little one from time to time and I'd best not find her depressed to any extent, or pregnant. Chaio, Florence, and keep the Faith."

MYRTLE, STOUT AND JOLLY, PRIESTESS OF HOLLY

Henry was laying in bed with his usual raging hard-on giving new meaning to the phrase, "brown eyed handsome man." He motioned for Myrtle to get back in bed but she replied, "Looks delicious, darling, but you're going to have to fly solo. This old bitch has got turkeys to cook, hams to clove, pies to bake, and mistletoe to be hung. There's going to be a whole lot of kissing going on. I want everyone to have their tongues down each other's throats. Christmas lust with a tad of gluttony on the side. Everything's got to be too much. Christmas overkill."

"I love you, bitch," replied Henry, "You're like Chaucer's Wife of Bath,"

"Henry, you know I don't read that shit."

"The Wife is the original party girl. In the story she sits around in a group of men and details every dirty trick she ever pulled on her husbands. Then she has the balls to say, 'I am available'. Myrt, you sure you can't stop a bit and throw me some ass?"

"If Santa wants to come down my chimney he'll just have to wait."

She reached over and tongued him in the mouth, saying, "Remember the Alamo, baby." She then lightly encircled his cock with her fingers, saying, "Anticipation is sweet, baby." He called her a cockteaser, and she replied, "You know it, honey."

And Myrtle left the room in an avalanche of lavender between her tits, thighs, and her jolly, fat neck. She went into her fifty thousand dollar, professional kitchen to begin her alchemy. Not for Myrtle, the pert caterer in a white uniform with a peppermint smile. She put the turkeys and hams first and then began to boil massive amounts of yams and potatoes. Then she did the trays of cornbread stuffing, her own special recipe with mushrooms, apple slices, onions, celery, and boiled eggs. Then the macaroni and cheese and an assortment of vegetables came after baking the pies of mincemeat, pumpkin, cherry, and apple. She also managed to bake rolls and bread from scratch. Her liquor cabinet rivaled that of any five star hotel. Rare cheeses and pates were also in evidence.

She thought to herself, "Float like a butterfly: sting like a bee. Ali was right."

Myrtle loved life. She loved cock, she loved food and liquor, and she loved the good times. Life was not a skate from one tragedy to the next. Life was a fun fest of pleasure and abundance. She wanted to enthrall the brave and the strong and to nourish the weak and meek souls too timid to take what they deserved from life. Christmas was her day. She decorated the fire places and tables and halls with greenery, elves, angels, and candles.

Her Christmas tree, a Spanish pinion, lay on its side in the living room festooned with colored Italian lights glittering like heart beats, bubble lights throbbing with joy, and small miniatures of silk red birds and little squirrels crawled amongst the branches. Angel hair like a fine spider's web was pulled over the entire ensemble. Christmas music like Bing Crosby, the Supremes, Lou Rawls, Louie Armstrong, and Lena Horn rang out throughout the house. As the guests moved throughout the house each stopped and pondered the tree.

What did it mean? Was it sad? Even Myrtle didn't know or care to know. It was simply the flow of life, unspeakably beautiful and unspeakably sad all at once.

Her guests for the size of the feast were comparatively small in number and included Gladys and her husband, Clive, and Lavinia and Bertie. Each person she greeted at the door with hugs, kisses, and exclamations of joy. "Come on in. Get your asses in here right now before you perish from starvation or cold. Don't stop until you're toasted and bloated. I mean it!"

Gladys came dressed as an elf in red and green leotard and tights and had sewn sleigh bells to her tits. Myrtle laughed, and said of the bells, "Why'd you stop there? Why not make it the Blessed Trinity?"

"That would have been stating the obvious," replied Gladys with a lush smile and a wink.

Myrtle roared with laughter. "Bitch, that was funny. Now get along to the buffet. If you don't leave here two sizes larger my mission is a failure!"

"Myrt, you did all this?"

"Sure, babe. Who else I don't have a lot of servants."

"You seen Lavinia?"

"She's probably leading Bertie in on a leash."

"Lovers and lap dogs," quipped Gladys. "Myrt, what do you think love is in all honesty?"

Myrtle replied, "One of two things. A contract for contentment or a contract for misery. Either one."

"Which do you prefer?" asked Gladys.

"Look at Henry and see if you can figure that one out, Gladys."

Lavinia then walked over. "What up, bitches? Where's the Stoli, Myrt?"

"At the bar. You like the music, Lavinia?"

"Myrt, I think we should all get down. Shake the fat: that's where it's at!" intoned Gladys.

"I'm not drunk enough but the idea has merit," replied Lavinia. "Just look at our husbands all banded together like out takes from Survivor."

"Three lads cast on the shore without a whore," quipped Myrtle.

"What do they talk about," pondered Gladys.

"Anything but us," Lavinia replied drily.

"And why not us?" asked Myrtle.

"Because then they'd be pale, or at least, Bertie would."

"Where'd you get all these duds, Myrt?" asked Lavinia tossing her head in the direction of Myrtle's guests. "They look like the other couple on 'Whose Afraid of Virginia Woolf'. You know, Sandy Dennis and George Segal."

"They're neighbors. Good simple folk. I like them. Don't fuck with them, Lavinia, or I'll tear your tits off such as they are."

"It's Christmas and I'm sentimental about Christmas. I'll be nice even if it doesn't come easy," said Lavinia.

"Lavinia, you're all in black. Why so funereal?" inquired Gladys.

"I'm losing weight and want the world to know it," she replied.

"How much so far, babes?" asked Myrtle.

"Forty pounds. My publicist says I should have a better image."

"Your publicist?"

"Yes," replied Lavinia. "A guy named Armand. "And he told me to change my love scene into a threesome, the heroine and two men."

"Now that sure aint Jackie Collins," quipped Myrtle. "Did you do it?"

"Why not? I'm a purveyor of popular culture not Shakespeare. Armand said it wasn't believable that my lover would go completely straight. I have to meet him halfway in more ways than one," laughed Lavinia.

"Was it hard to write?" asked Gladys.

"No, not really once you get the angles down," laughed Lavinia.

"You amaze us!" they said together.

"Just show me the money as the saying goes," replied Lavinia. "What the hell could the husbands be talking about. Think I'll go over."

"Very well. Report back," said Myrtle drily.

"Probably twat size and bedroom eyes. I shall see. Bye for now."

As Lavinia walked over to them there was now a graceful sway in her still ripe, full hips and she tossed her sandy brown hair back like a lion's mane. Her cheekbones were more prominent and her mean cat eyes had a glint of ferocity in them. The cleft on her chin was a tad androgynous and arresting in appearance. Her gait suggested to men the hunger and viciousness of a cougar. Albert had noticed a change in her bed time manner, at once more disdainful and more passionate. She had forsaken the long ago Birkenstocks for flashier designer shoes such as black ankle high stiletto boots or red patent leather high heeled pumps.

"What up, Bertie. You boys talking about golf and ticker tape. Put the stocks in a box. The bitch is here."

"No, we're talking about destiny versus free will, a kind of nature versus nurture thing," replied Henry, Myrtle's husband. "I gave a job to a gang banger the other day though he did have a college degree. You know, affirmative action, and I get a tax break at the end of the year."

Lavinia felt her tongue snake out and slide over her bottom lip, and she thought to herself, "Damn, my Bertie is such a slug and Henry's so damn good looking."

As if Bertie could hear her thought he slumped even lower into himself like a deflated parachute.

"So do you think he'll make it, Bertie," she said as if to placate him for her rude thought.

"Well, some of these young negroes do rather well if given a chance."

"So, free will exists. Is that what you're saying, Bertie? And it's African American not negro, dear."

Clive, Gladys's husband replied, "Free will exists for some people and not others, my dear."

"How so?" she queried.

"Third world countries. Ruwanda. The untouchables in India and the Jews in Nazi Germany. Think they had free will, Lavinia?" Clive was tall and thin, a corporate angel of a man who just missed being handsome by a fraction.

Lavinia squinted her eyes and fancied that he was "okay" in the right light. Then she thought to herself, "What the fuck's wrong with you, Lavinia? Art is all that really matters."

"Clive, anyone of them could become great. Anything's possible."

"Could, but have they? If elephants had wings and angels could fuck," said Henry.

"It's still possible. Look at Ghandi. He came from nothing and he became a great man."

"Or for that matter, look at you three bitches," interjected Henry, "You didn't have jack shit before you met us. Three little Cinderella's. Anything can happen. 'Nothing is written', to quote T. E. Lawrence."

"I take umbrage to that remark, Henry. I had my education. I had my mind. Money can't buy a sharp, incisive mind," she replied.

"On the contrary, money buys books, and books build minds. Hell, even beauty isn't free. You've got to have a gym membership."

"I have never met such a cynical person!" snapped Lavinia.

"Money is destiny, my pretty. If you're lying in the gutter with dust on your balls, air in your stomach and no roof over your head you're not going to write War and Peace or build a bridge. You're going to piss off and die. Greatness comes to those who have had the opportunity to develop it! If we were all created equal, I dare say we'd all be happy and rich. Free will exists but it needs a little push!" said Henry.

"Bertie, what do you say?" she asked.

"Well, I think you're both right in your own way. And besides, philosophy is not my area. Give me some numbers and I'm your man."

"You're such a numb nuts," she snapped.

Henry replied, "He's not a numb nuts, Lavinia. He's a no nuts since you cut 'em both off! Do you keep them in a glass jar at home like pickled eggs?"

"Bertie! Do not let this man insult me! He insulted you too. Do something! I demand you crack him in the face!"

Myrtle as if sensing the tenseness in the air came over. She burst into the circle with drunken kisses and embraces and even tongued Bertie in the ear.

"Whoops, wrong husband. Sorry, Lavinia. Now everybody just get your fat asses over to the dance floor tout de suite. I aint hearing no arguments. Now get! Just get! And stop your damn caterwauling! And look at you people. Empty drink glasses. That's just unseemly at my party! Now, come along. No exceptions!"

Everyone, including Lavinia and Henry, did as told and Gladys and Myrtle took to the floor to the Weather Girls' song "It's Raining Men."

They bumped. They grinded. They embarrassed the young people with their lusty dance rendition. At the end they tongued each other passionately in the mouth.

"What the fuck was that?" asked Lavinia.

"Just messing with their heads. Besides I bet they can't be sure of what they saw with the stobe light going," laughed Myrtle.

"Where'd you get the disco ball, Myrtle?" she asked.

"Got it at a flea market, Lavinia. Same place I got these," with that Myrtle flashed Lavinia showing her the red and gold tassels on her tits.

"Henry just loves this shit."

"You're a pill, Myrtle."

"Yes, Lavinia, I sure as hell am. Now I'm going to check the buffet and the liquor cabinet. That mousy little bitch from next door nearly drank a fifth of my best four malt scotch. I may check on her after I've got things squared away. Lavinia, circulate, envelope, devour. Do what you do best, my sweet."

Myrtle found her hapless guest slumped over the toilet sobbing. Rivulets of vomit ran down the sides of her mouth and clumps of it were in her hair. Her eyes were puffed out like two Portobello mushrooms.

"What's the matter, sweetie, too much of the grape?" she said gently tucking a strand of hair behind her ear.

"I'm a goddamned alcoholic. My children don't respect me and Tom hates me. He's never home."

"Are you about through with this toilet, honey. I'm going to get you all cleaned up and put you in the shower and give you one of my "thin" dresses. Then we can have a little talk. I'm going to order a pot of Earl Grey and some English shortbread cookies from my servant. You just leave everything to Old Myrt. I'll fix you right up."

After listening to Adelaide's sad and mirthless tale for about an hour Myrtle intervened.

"You know, Adelaide, everyone says alcoholism is a disease. What it really is is an unhappiness in the soul, a tumult in your heart, a failure to thrive. Don't answer me but it is my guess that your fondest wish is to be a good wife and mother. Don't answer, babes, I know. But I'm going to tell you that that dream is not a big enough dream for a grown woman. All that giving and nothing back could make anyone ill, honey. You got to have your own dream separate from your family. Is there anything you wanted to be when you were young?"

"I wanted to be a ballerina but I'm way too old for that now."

"You aint dead yet, honey, and it's never too late. I have interests myself. I'm a clothing designer. Just for myself now but who knows where it will lead. Everyone must have a dream, baby, or your light will go out."

"But you're different, Myrtle. You're stronger than I am."

"I'm stronger because I will myself to be stronger, babes. You've got to grab life, gorge yourself on it, conquer it! Because it doesn't last. Love yourself, honey. What are you, Lucretia Borgia or a prison matron at Auschwitz? You deserve to have a blast. I know you do!"

"I just can't help myself," sobbed Adelaide.

"Actually, you're the only one who can. Aint nobody strong enough to carry another person's soul. You ask to much of your Tom. Quit being a fucking baby. Get your ass some help tout de suite!"

"You make it sound so black and white."

"That's because it is! Now eat, drink the tea and think on what I've said. I'm going to leave you here now to do some pondering. If you need a ride home, my driver will take you."

When Myrtle got back the party was dissolving slowly. She saw Lavinia over in the corner crushing Bertie's spirit or so she assumed. Then she thought of Lavinia, "The old gal's beginning to look pretty good in a Barbra Streisand kind of way."

Then she went around picking up stray plates and ash trays. It was then she saw something that gave her pause. It was Gladys straddling her husband, dry humping him, and she saw a flash of pink that indicated Henry's dick was out. She stopped still and stood at the door waiting for the vitriol to rise. Henry's left eye caught her image and he pushed Gladys off his lap.

"It's not what it looks like, baby," he stammered.

"And, what does it look like, Henry, the Charge of the Light Brigade? Gladys, don't say a word. Get your ass in the kitchen. I'll deal with you then!"

Gladys shot out of the room like an extra fast bullet.

"Myrt. I was drunk. Didn't know what the fuck I was doing. She doesn't mean anything to me. It's you I love. Baby, please."

"NEVER IN OUR HOUSE, HENRY. I told you and told you, and still you fuck up, excuse the expression. And where's the sleigh bell missing from Gladys costume?"

Wordlessly Henry spit it out. "What were you going to do ring 'Jingle Bells' as you fucked her?"

"You know I'd fuck a lawn ornament if I was drunk. It didn't mean anything, I'm so, so sorry, Myrt. I can make it up to you."

"A bauble, and an all night fuck, you cocksucker," replied Myrtle.

"Tonight's the night. I'll get the bauble tomorrow. Okay, baby?"

"Better than never, motherfucker. I ought to cut off your damn nuts so you could be one of the nuns in the Our Sister of the Impending Chastity nunnery. Fortunately for you, Henry, I still have a use for them."

"I love you, Baby," he replied.

"Me, too, sweetie," she replied.

Then Myrtle found Gladys in the kitchen slumped over a luke warm cup of coffee. Her face was ashen pale. She took a butcher knife from its wooden holder and placed it on the counter.

"You know, Gladys, in Africa they have little ritual called female circumcision. They claim it makes for faithful wives. Why are you so pale? Oh, you thought…" and Myrtle burst out in laughter.

"Actually, I'd use this straight razor from my purse for that particular activity, Gladys, not the butcher knife. Too unwieldy."

"Myrt, that's a concealed weapon," said Gladys with a quiver in her voice.

"Course it is, and so is my cunt. I've got a thing about muggers, Gladdy. They scare me. What would you have me do in that situation, pray?"

"Myrt, I had no idea you were so violent."

"Violent, no. I'm gentle as a lamb. I haven't used it on you have I?"

"No."

"But I also tell you I'd never inform Clive of your little adventures, or I don't think I would."

"Oh, Myrt, don't. He'd divorce me and I'm too old and fat for the typing pool. Please, please don't."

"Well, clearly, I can't do that. Wouldn't want to do that to my good good friend, Gladys. How's that hunky gardener of yours. I'd sure like to get some of my sticky on that man."

"But I love him."

"Now you've got the point, Gladdy. I love my Henry and I protect what is mine."

"I never knew you were so rough, Myrt."

"And you never crossed me before either, did you?"

"No."

"Are we clear in ourselves, girl friend?" asked Myrtle.

"Yes, Myrt."

"Good, because I love you to bits, babes.

As Gladys got up to leave she noted her legs and arms felt watery and weak but her heart was warm as the sun.

THE BODY BEAUTIFUL

It was the usual Friday at Myrtle's and the girls were painting the world with vitriol and honey in alternating fashion. Then out of the blue, Myrtle blew on a toy whistle and dramatically held up two plastic cards in the air.

"Girls, these cards have your names on them, a little gift from your old girl friend, Myrt."

"Oh, goodie, are they Nieman Marcus cards?" asked Gladys.

"Why the drama?" asked Lavinia.

"Because I like it, bitch," replied Myrtle. "Actually they're two Bally's cards at fifteenth and Walnut, and the trainer's name is on the name card I've clipped to the plastic. A good looking, black gay guy named Dante."

"What the hell, Myrt. I've already lost forty pounds," said Lavinia.

"But it still jiggles, babe. Must be jelly 'cause jam don't shake like that."

"I don't want to go, Myrt. I hate exercise," whined Gladys. "Besides Enrtique likes me just like I am."

"You're so beautiful, you'd rule the world if you were thin, Gladys," replied Myrtle.

"I don't want to rule the world. I only want to fuck, eat, and spend money," said Gladys.

"You're so vegetative, Gladys. Eat, sleep, fuck. Just like an animal only you don't procreate," observed Lavinia.

"I should have your children, Lavinia. At least they'd be raised by a human," replied Gladys.

"Bitch, I'm going to shove my fist up your cunt, complete with diamond ring."

"Enough, girls," replied Myrtle. "We're not gay men. Now listen, we're all good looking. We just need a little work. Even the playing field with all the skinny bitches in this world. We could stand some improvement."

"Look, Myrt, if we're so bad off why do we even have men? You think it's pity fucking?" asked Gladys.

"Decidedly not," replied Myrtle. "It's the smell. Men can smell sex plus the thought of our legs rubbing together all the time gets them hot."

"You really think that's the reason why?" asked Lavinia.

"Definitely. Now I've got leotards for the both of you. Lavinia, yours is red: Gladys, yours is the blue one. Put them on, girls and let's go to the hall mirror. I mean it, bitches. Do it if you expect to leave here alive. I've already got mine on under my clothes, and it isn't a pretty sight."

The girls reluctantly put on the gym clothes.

"Myrt, did you have to give us thongs?" asked Gladys.

"Sure did. Now what do you see girls?"

Lavinia cupped her small sized, sagging tits and said, "I see 'The Fall of the House of Usher'".

Gladys burst into gales of laughter and said, "I see 'Naked Lunch'".

Then Lavinia laughed. Of course Myrtle didn't get it, but she said, "I've got a second brain in my lower back just like a Brontosaurus to control my ass and legs, and my tits are on a pulley system to hold them up! Girls, we need some self improvement."

"I'm in," said Lavinia.

"Me too," said Gladys.

"Let's feast today and starve tomorrow. 'Life is a banquet and most poor bastards are starving.' I heard this in a movie. We're having filet mignon wrapped in bacon, baked potatoes and sour cream, asparagus tips in hollandaise sauce, dinner rolls and quacamole and chips to start. For desert were having strawberry tarts with whipped cream. And I've chilled four bottles of Mum's champagne to stimulate our brains. Can I get an amen?"

"Well, amen, bitch," said Lavinia.

"Ditto," said Gladys.

The next morning Myrtle waddled into the gym and asked the lithe parrot of a girl to show her the machines. After finishing the girl asked how else she might help Myrtle.

"Nothing else," replied Myrtle. "Just keep on being your sweet self, honey."

Inside Myrtle had a wrathful thought, "Shove that elliptical machine up your ass, Miss Scarlet O'Hara."

While working on the machines her heart pushed up into her throat, and her arms and legs felt heavy like vats of lead.

She thought, "Moving fat is like moving a fucking herd of cattle across the desert."

Then Gladys came in wearing her scarlet thong Myrtle gave her. Dante, the black trainer came over and asked if the "ladies" were ready for their training session to which they replied in the affirmative.

Gladys noted the sensual snarl of his lips and the rippling of his abs beneath his tee shirt and her tongue involuntarily snaked out across her full, pouty lips.

"Maybe he's not gay all the way," she thought, and then caught the arch of Myrtle's eyebrow.

"Always judging," she thought, and Myrtle's telepathic reply was unprintable.

The trainer noted that Myrtle's problematic area was her large waist and gave her floor exercises, and demonstrations on the waist trimming machines. With Gladys he concentrated on thigh and hip reducing machines. As mentioned before, Gladys was perfectly in proportion. It was a rank, assertive, rambunctious beauty of the sort gay men find especially offensive. She was a "too much" dolly. He had the gay men's aversion to fat, or more politely, cellulite.

He was secretly disgusted at our robust duo and thought to himself, "No wonder I'm gay. The smell's enough to knock a buzzard off a shit wagon. Don't they ever douche?"

Then he showed them both the machines for the upper arms and inner thighs, "Those legs rubbing together all the time just can't be good," he thought," quietly running his hand over his muscled stomach as if to assure himself of his own pulchritude.

After the session they went to the juice bar and had two carrot and celery juices and Myrtle remarked, "This shit's likely to kill me. Clear out all the cholesterol at once and give me a heart attack."

"You only say that because it aint eighty proof," laughed Gladys. Then letting her eyes roll lazily over Dante as he instructed a sparrow of a girl on the elliptical machine, she remarked idly to Myrtle, "I wonder if I could turn him."

"They don't change sides, Gladys. They're hard wired for it."

"Clive says 'Nothing is written".

"I say it is. Look at the manafacturer's stamp on his forehead. It says 'seriously gay'. Girl, stay away from this shit."

"I wonder if it's true?" replied Gladys.

"What's true?"

"Once you go black you never go back," replied Gladys.

"Clive, his Republican Ass Ship, would whip the hell out of you if you ever did a black man. Much less a gay black man."

"Who says Clive has to know? You know I'm not prejudiced. Besides, this is just a fantasy."

"Your fantasies have a way of coming true, Gladys."

"You mean you think I could do it?"

"How the hell do I know? I don't know anything about gays. Just heard they were dedicated. That's all."

"Care to make it interesting, Myrtle?"

"Oh, shit."

"A case of Jameison says I can."

"All right, you crazy bitch. Three months."

"Make if four. I'm an artist. I take my time."

"Four it is. We're both going to fry in hell for this."

"Homosexuality is a sin, Myrt. Even the Bible says so."

"Being a fucking bitch is also a sin, Gladys though the Bible doesn't directly say so. Read between the lines."

"We'll worry about hell when we get there. Lest you forget, God is a man."

"Not a man, idiot, a Spirit. God doesn't care about pussy, Gladys."

"Who says so? He made twats didn't he?"

"Your logic is infallible, my girl," said Myrtle.

"I've got it all planned. First, I'll take him to Le Bec Fin for lunch. No self respecting gay will turn down a free, expensive meal. Then I'll start buying him designer cologne, shirts, and jewelry. Then I'll tell him about Enrique and me with the emphasis on Enrique. I'll get really graffic. Then soon I'll be sucking dick in the men's room right shortly, verily I say unto you."

"You said fuck him," replied Myrtle.

"I did not, bitch. Turning means any act with a straight woman. Dante, can you come here a minute. I need additional instruction." And she snapped her fingers.

He came over and she winked at Myrtle,

"Dante, I need to be checked out on the machines on this floor. Please excuse my friend, Myrtle. She's all pooped out now, and has to go home and make herself a little salad. Toodleloo, dear. Be seeing you!"

Myrtle laughed and took her fat ass home. In the months following they went to the gum religiously and adhered to a strict health diet, never wavering, and the inches began to slowly come off. Lavinia, the most competitive of the three, went more often, worked out more strenuously, and put herself on a more Spartan diet.

In the end, she became a woman of today, lean, lithe, and sculpted. And the girls were glad for her and not sad for themselves as she had wished.

After a four month period, Myrtle noticed a change in Dante's behavior. He stood closer to Gladys and frequently came over to gossip with her when she was working out. He hung on her every word and laughed at all her jokes, particularly those about Clive. And he often added ones of his own, faint references to penile size and things of this ilk.

Then one day while on her way to shower Myrtle heard faint moaning and grunting sounds coming from the men's locker room, and she went to investigate.

"What the hell. I'll just tell them I'm old and confused if they freak," she told herself.

Upon entering she saw Gladys down on her knees sucking off Dante vigorously while another good looking gay men jerked off across from them. When she was finished, she held out her arms to the other guy, and said, "Come to Mama," which he did.

Upon questioning later, Gladys revealed that the other man was Dante's boy friend, Pete.

"Two, two, two, mens in one," quipped Myrtle, who further said, "Drive me to the liquor store. You win, bitch."

It will be noted that Gladys was using condoms on her two friends. A few days later they read in the Inquirer that the boy friend had killed Dante in a fit of passion. Gladys cried and cried and blamed herself to a degree.

"He was so sweet, honest and gentle, Myrtle. I think I loved him and he wrote me sonnets, Myrtle, sonnets. I think maybe Pete just got jealous."

"You think he went to heaven, Gladys?"

"Oh, definitely. All that rhyming, meter and imagery. Such talent, and girl friend, such a dick!"

LAVINIA, UP TO NO GOOD

While Myrtle and Gladys were scandalizing Bally's gym, grunting and throbbing at the machines, and flirting with every man gay or straight, Lavinia was also up to no good. Quel sorprese! She began to sample fruit from the man tree, starting with her publicist, Armand. The first and most notable of her conquests was this bookish, balding mogul who smelled like a goat, walked like an ape, and had words which fled from his tongue like rain water dripping from a roof. Lavinia, was more narrow, selective and discreet in her sampling than Gladys. Subtly sexy, he was like a haiku hidden in a fortune cookie. He inflamed our Mistress of the Mists.

One day she came to his office dressed in a black leather mini skirt, see through, black organza blouse, and thigh high patent leather boots.

"Armand," she said, "What have you done for me lately?"

He looked up startled from his papers on his desk, and replied, "Lavinia, you starled me. Where's Estelle? I didn't hear you come in."

"I sent her home for the afternoon. We have to get something straight between us."

"If it's about your commission, I've given you a very fair deal for a first time novel, and Random House is looking. What do you mean, I'm not doing enough?"

Lavinia, went over to his desk, and removed his glasses setting them on the outer edge of his desk. She then cleared the stack of papers from his desk with one sweep of her arm and then she perched atop his desk and spread her legs revealing a shocking absence of underwear. Her luscious pearl was right at his eye level, and she saw the play of a smile on his lips.

"Lavinia, I knew you'd do this sooner or later."

"I'm that transparent, am I?"

"Darling, I'm an agent. I eat little girls like you for breakfast."

"Then eat me now, Armand," she replied.

And, he did. Long, slow, and surely. Lavinia shrieked and pushed her sex more harshly into his mouth and then her back snapped back in one violent spasm as she practically fell from consciousness. He disengaged himself from her, slowly removing his own clothes and hers.

His nakedness revealed a surprisingly supple, powerful body and a prodigious male instrument.

"What do you want next, baby? Command me, Lavinia."

And she replied, "I want to ride you like Lilith." He nodded in assent and took in her long, tense body, a long stemmed white rose with thorns.

He noted her small, firm tits looking like two fresh, ripe nectarines.

She sat on him. She lurched and she crawled. She wrecked him and herself. When she was done he had a bite mark on his chest, and bloody scratch marks from her long red nails.

"Damn, baby. Are you a succubus?"

"Practically. You could say that."

"I'm going to have to stay away from home for a week so Laura won't see these."

"Tell me about wifey-poo," replied Lavinia.

"No, dice, baby, I don't talk about my wife."

"Tell me this, is she fat?"

"No, she's your size but not your soul such as it is," he replied.

"Don't look a gift horse in the mouth, fucker," she intoned.

"Don't intend to. Look, Lavinia, I like you and would like to keep mixing business and pleasure if that's agreeable to you. I count myself lucky to know you."

"It is agreeable to me, Armand. Want me to put some brandy on your scratches to kind of sterilize them," she said offering her ever present silver flask to him.

"No, but I bet you'd really like that. I have my own remedies. AKA, the emergency ward. Just kidding, baby, but, no."

A slight smile creased her face as she dressed in silence. She was certain this man perceived her in a way that Bertie never could. Bertie was a puppy dog and this man was a shark. A shark who understood lust, and power, and women. He was a man she could love and therefore, dangerous to her heart or what passed for one.

He brushed her lip with one finger and whispered, the word, "until" into her ear. Then he closed the door and went back to his papers. As she let herself out, she fell into the outside world like a deer blinded by headlights.

As the months wore on and on, she began to perceive him as "hers", and the wife as the "other woman". He never lied, made promises, or once mentioned the word, "love." But Lavinia wove that word into her hard, thorny heart, and she drank him like a well on the desert. He drank of her, too, but he was immune.

The clear, white pearlescent goodness of his wife still dominated his heart. The love of his wife and children was of utmost importance to him. He considered Lavinia a dangerous and exotic animal not a woman to keep. She was a woman to make his blood boil, a woman powerful enough to blot out the whole goddamned world when she was with him. It was a stolen moment not a life.

Imagine his chagrin and surprise when Lavinia told him she was leaving Bertie so they could be together. He saw the passion in her eyes and the conviction that he, too, felt the same. He informed her that it was not so and then saw horrible tabloid pictures flash in those eyes. Pictures of a dismembered wife and dead children. He gasped, and reached out to Lavinia to comfort her. Lavinia took it all in in slience but the rage imploded in her face. He saw it and was afraid like he had never been before. He was afraid for his family and for his business arrangements with her. Her books were flying off the shelves. She was the darling of frustrated housewives everywhere.

As if reading his mind, Lavinia gently took his face in her hands, and peered into his eyes. He could not read her expression. She said dispassionately, "Listen, Armand, get over yourself. Not even you are worth that. I kill souls, baby, not corporeal beings, you can go to jail for that. Think I want to go to prison and have some damn bull dyke sitting on my face for the rest of my natural life? No, baby, I am not that crazy! I won't harm your fucking family, and yes, we're still partners. Money is thicker than blood."

With those words she slammed out of the room pausing in the doorway to say these words, "Oh, yes, baby. Thanks for the good times. It was a blast! Chaio!"

Armand went home and packed up his family for an extended six month stay in Europe, a vacation he called it. When the family got back he was ecstatic. Things were going so well at home. The sales of Lavinia's books were through the roof and Lavinia was behaving so professionally, and friendly to him. It just made his heart glad. Things had worked out well, or so he thought.

But, our girl, as anyone knows just hated to lose. She soon made it her business to know where his children went to school, and his wife, Laura's daily schedule, all her comings and goings.

One day Lavinia just happened to be in Susanah Foo's, an upscale Chinese restaurant, where Laura and her girlfriends were having lunch.

Casually she went over to Laura's table and introduced herself saying she was a business associate and old friend of her husband, Armand, and had something to discuss with her. There was a momentary silence at the table in which case Lavinia raised her hand saying, "It's nothing important. I assure you. Relax, enjoy your meal, ladies. See you later, Laura." Laura flinched the tiniest bit upon hearing her name on the lips of a total stranger. This was not lost on Lavinia.

"So what did you want to tell me?" asked Laura.

Lavinia suggested she sit down and get "comfortable" which she did.

Then Lavinia coldly and analytically told her the nature of her visit.

The woman turned white, fought back tears, and grasped the edge of the table like a ship wreck victim holds onto the side of a sinking ship.

Lavinia smiled and patted her hand in a grandmotherly fashion, saying,

"And darling, this was not the first time, nor will it be the last. It's not that he doesn't love you. He told me he loves you very much. It's just that he can't keep it in his pants. That's the long and the short of it. No pun intended."

Laura stood up suddenly knocking over her chair, and Lavinia, as well, stood up abruptly, grasping her forearm harshly with her long, sharp nails. Lavinia stared into her eyes and said coldly, "Laura you are not leaving just yet. I am not through with you. Sit down, or I will make you sit down. Do you want me to make a scene here because I will, believe me, dear."

The woman, somewhat afraid sat back down.

"Tonight, you will go home and you will wear these things, my lingerie and shoes. We are the same size, you see. And you will do as I do, or have done. First I sit on his face. Armand is a real pussy hound, my dear. Then you sit on him and ride real rough, and give him little love bites and rake him with your nails. Bring blood. Then you say nothing. Act as if it's perfectly normal, something you always do. Watch his eyes when he sees you wearing my things. Do not cry. Do not accuse. Do not weaken in any way. Look I know you're pissed, honey, and have a right to be. But revenge is a dish best served cold as they say. Shouting, and crying and making a scene are totally ineffective. If you do what I suggest he'll be too damned afraid to fuck you over again. Show your claws girls, but don't de-nut him. Even I would not recommend that. Men respect women with balls. He'll love you even more now, and respect you too. And he does love you, Laura. That I know. Will you do what I say?"

Laura looked at Lavinia in a clear, gray eyed way, cat to cat, and said,

"Yes, I will do it just like you say. Don't ever let me see you again, Lavinia."

"Not a glimpse," said Lavinia with a wide smile straightening Laura's collar like her dear mother.

That night after his ordeal Armand heard Lavinia's words come back to haunt him.

"I kill souls, baby, not corporeal bodies because you go to jail for that."

Watching her in their room that night, the devil smiled, and thought to himself, "Masterful, Lavinia, masterful."

COUGARS AND GIGILOS

"Well, Myrt, why are we all dressed to the nines at seven at night? What is your big surprise this time?" asked Gladys.

"Yeah, what the hell's going on? Bertie thinks I'm cheating on him and this time I'm not. It's pissing me off," said Lavinia.

"Well, girls, we are going to have a little adventure. Tonight we are going to the Academy of Social Chance on Sampson Street, where cougars and gigolos intersect for fun and profit! Then later we'll have a little pajama party, Fredericks's of Hollywood and all that shit. I've hired a photographer. We'll pretend we're lezzies. Give the husbands something to jerk off to!" replied Myrtle.

"First off, why are we going to that place? We never have to pay for it, and aren't we a little old for a pajama party?" said Lavinia.

"We aint too old for either," replied Myrtle. "Where's you sense of fun, Lavinia?"

"It seems like a capital idea. I've never met a real gigilo except for Richard Gere in 'American Gigilo' and I never actually met him. What will we call our pajama party, Myrt? Said Gladys.

"I suggest Pussy Galore," replied Lavinia.

Myrtle laughed and said, "That's a damn sight better than Tit for Tat!"

"What can I say?" said Lavinia stretching her arms out in a gesture of supplication. "And why are we doing this, Myrt?"

"To fuck with their heads and because I just need something to do on Halloween. Conchita's at a class party with Henry."

"What is it again, Myrt?" asked Lavinia.

"It's a social club for ballroom dancing with fucking and drinking on the side…for a price," she replied. "Cougars and gigolos, and darling, we are the cougars."

"But like I said, we don't need to pay for it. At least not in dollars and cents," replied Lavinia.

"I know, silly. It's a goof. Don't you get it? We get to role play and never pay. Oops! I'm rhyming."

"Well, I guess that does have some merit. What do you say, Gladys?" asked Lavinia.

"I'm laughing my damn ass off,' replied Gladys.

"See? See what I mean? Girls, has old Myrt ever steered you wrong? I want to show off my new waist line. For once I don't look pregnant with child."

"If you were it'd be immaculate conception. You aint seen the red river in a good seven years, Myrt." Said Lavinia.

"True. But what the hell, girls. I'm fabulous!"

And she was. They all were. Myrtle gleamed like a jubilant star in a burmished gold Vera sheath and her signature high, strappie "Jimmy" shoes. Her skin, milk white, with a splattering of minutely orange freckles glowed with good health due to careful dieting and little snip, snip from the plastic surgeon.

Gladys was a voluptuous red cherry though not round, her tiny waist in stark bas relief to her pungent, omnipresent, highly toned ass. She wore her mink stole with an air of joie de vivre, a small defiance to the forces of woe and misery.

Lavinia, in black and panther like, would later glide into the club leading with the arc of her sharp, prominent hip bones, trailing her ass behind like fifteen pounds of fresh meat. She had about her the sense of the feral and dangerous. The other two, Myrtle and Gladys, radiated warmth and comfort, and easy, abundant, rank sexual power. Their luminous jewels glittered in the night air like distant stars in the darkening sky. They were three pearls thrown to swine and they were well aware of it. Clearly they were women of means, the favorite meat of gigolos seeking to feed.

Their driver pulled up to the club at seven forty-five with instructions to stand by. After drinking two full bottles of champagne in the limo on the way over our girls were in quite the jovial mood upon arrival. A dark skinned, gray haired Italian man named Don Marco welcomed them to the club, taking their wraps and collecting the cover charge which was exorbitant.

"Dues have sure gone up since our last girls scout meeting, Myrtle,"Lavinia remarked.

"Duly noted," replied Myrtle.

"Damn, he's pretty," commented Gladys.

"You can look but you better not touch,
Gonna take an ocean of calamine lotion,
You'll be scratching like a hound
The minute he comes around.
Poison ivy, Poison Ivy, Poison ivy-ee," countered Myrtle.

"That's a oldie," replied Gladys.

"As, are you, dear. Lest you forget," replied Myrtle.

"Will you look at these people," said Lavinia. "Amazing."

The lizard skinned, spry old cougars were clinging passionately to dazed young men with rippling thighs and cleft chins. Sounds of the rhumba, the cha-cha, the tango, and the meringue emanated from the sound system, and colored skirts rippled as if caught in a wind.

"The men remind me of movie star doubles. Look at Bobby De Niro over there. Dibs. Who do you want, Myrtle?" asked Lavinia.

"I'll take the Don Ameche. He looks like he's got a good line, and Gladys, who do you want?"

"I like the Tony Franciosa. How do you propose we get them, Myrt?"

"Easy," interrupted Lavina. "Toward the middle or end of the evening we ask them to dance with us. We look richer than any of these old cunts in here. They'll come."

"You're such a bitch, Lavinia. Can't you see they're pathetic. I feel sorry for these old birds," replied Myrtle.

"You would," replied Lavina.

"It could be you one day, Lavinia."

"Oh yeah, Myrt. Like I'm going to be in here when I'm seventy-five in a wheelchair sucking dick!"

"You're too rough, babe. Tone it down," said Myrtle. "They're human beings. You've got to learn to pass as one yourself."

"You're right, Myrt. I'm just upset with Armand. He really fucked me over," she replied.

"Business wise?" asked Myrtle.

"No," replied Lavinia.

"I see. Well, the world's full of bastards, and they sure got some of them in here. Let's play a bit. Don't be so serious, honey."

"Okay, you're right, Myrt. I'll be single and an heiress. It's going to be oil money and I'm doing my primo Texas accent. Does that sound plausible to you?"

"They'd believe it if you said you were fucking Princess Grace of Monaco come to life again. I'm a rich widow, and lonely. Terribly lonely. Looking for love in all the wrong places, as the song goes," replied Myrtle.

"I'm a Siamese twin," piped in Gladys. "The one that got the money. My sister didn't get jack shit 'cause she pissed Daddy off. Wouldn't do him. Men love incest."

The girls sat back and watched the action as the night enfolded. Young and old were doing ball room dance and all were surprisingly skilled. The disco ball, like an over sized diamond, sent refracted light out onto the dance floor. The colored strobes gave the room the magenta aspect of a Fasbinder film.

"Wrinkles look better under purple light," commented Gladys as she idly stirred her strawberry daiquiri with a swizzle stick.

"I'm so drunk a pile of steaming, hot shit would look good to me now," interjected Lavinia who threw back a straight shot of Dewar's.

"You're depressed, baby," said Myrt. "How long since Armand?"

"Nine months and counting."

"Someone better will come along, sweetie."

"But I loved that fucker," replied Lavinia.

"But I bet you got even. I know you Lavinia," replied Myrtle.

"You could say that."

"Care to tell us, babes," said Myrtle.

"Not really. But from now on I want you to do my business with him, Myrtle. He's really pissed at me and I just don't want to talk to him."

"Okay you just tell me what you want me to say. I don't want that bastard to jerk you around any more," said Myrtle.

All the while the girls talked, countless young men came up to them and were politely and firmly rebuffed. The girls had selected their men and were waiting to read the ticker tape of their hearts to tell them when to make their moves. At one point Don Marco himself came over and asked them why they had not found anyone to their liking and if his men had done anything to displease them. He even added coyly, that his men were feeling, "rejected". He "implored" them to tell him how he might please them. The girls then told him of their requests and the men were sent over. There came over the Don's face a look of relief and avarice like an old time gangster movie in which Lee Van Cleef learns he has won the gang war and everyone else is dead. Myrtle got the Don Ameche: Lavinia got Bobby De Niro and Gladys got her Tony Franciosa. It was possibly just a wonderful evening.

Myrtle did not spill out her dreams and tell of her horrible life as a widow for she was playing a "merry" widow. She determined to get her date to talk about himself.

"So, Carlo," she intoned, "What's the best piece of ass you ever had?"

Unflustered he replied, "It hasn't happened until now, madam."

"Son of a bitch. You're good."

"Good, yes," replied Carlo who smiled revealing one gold tooth, His diamond cufflink gave off a spark of colored light as his arm snaked around her shoulder.

"Myrtle, you seem a mature woman, very wise. I'm going to make you very happy, darling."

"Honey," she replied as she winked and placed one hand on his knee, "You remind me of my late husband, Henry. Very delicious, if you know what I mean."

"I am definitely delicious, as are you, my lady," he said kissing her hand.

"Tell me about yourself, Carlo."

"Nothing to tell, madam. I exist, therefore I am."

"Do you think these are real?" she said pushing out her breasts.

"If God did not make them, I would be genuinely surprised."

"Oh, you are so good! I'd say you were made in heaven if I didn't know better."

There a dark disturbance and a wild mirth in his eyes, The gigilo was enjoying himself."No, not in heaven, madam. Definitely not."

And he burst out in laughter. Myrtle also laughed uproariously and punched him in the arm. Then Myrtle began to draw him out finding out his origins, his childhood, his meager hopes and dreams. Men whores like women whores dream of material things, corporeal things. It did not surprise her that he did not want to become an engineer, or a scientist. He lived in the NOW. He was a constantly evolving organism, a chameleon dedicated to becoming just what any woman dreamed he was. He was literally a man for all seasons. His dream was to survive, and to survive grandly. At first, he was uncomfortable talking about himself but after a while he was pleased that someone wanted to know more about him than just the dimension of his cock. The conversation went as follows.

"So, you're from Italy, Carlo?"

I am Sicilian. From a long line of soft men who liked to drink, gamble and womanize. We were not fit to deal with the other Sicilians: we were noblemen. True, as you have probably gathered I work for them but I am not that kind. The only thing I kill is flies around the dinner table."

"Do you enjoy it? This killing of flies?"

"Definitely," he said biting into the large olive in his martini.

"I myself like to kill cockroaches because I don't know why God invented them."

"I don't ever think I've heard a woman say anything like that."

"What have you heard women say, Carlo?"

"And you can't guess, my lovely?"

"They say," Myrtle replied, "that they don't have love in their lives and that their men don't understand them. And the honest ones just say 'how much?' Am I right?"

"You're right, Myrtle. They're all terribly sad like neglected lawn mowers sitting on a beautiful lawn. Something tells me you are not neglected. No man would ever dare."

"No, no man would, you're right Carlo."

"What would you like to say about yourself, Myrtle?"

"I like hot sauce, baby. Lots of it. Were you poor, Carlo?"

"Yes."

"Was your childhood happy?"

"Not especially. I had eight brothers and sisters. Catholics to the end, my mom, and pop. We ate pizza dough slathered with tomato sauce and bits of mozzarella but the red wine always flowed particularly for poppa. I cannot eat pizza to this day."

"What did you do for Christmas, Carlo?"

"Go to church and thank God for our happy lives."

"Did you mean it?"

"Altar boys always mean it, baby. Life has not always been pleasant but it is good now. I am happy in what I do. It is my gift."

"You are an engineer of pussy."

"Well said, Myrtle. Now may I hear about you?"

"No, you may not. I'm just a housewife, Carlo. You are the exotic one, most definitely."

At that point, Gladys' date burst out with, "No shit, a Siamese twin. You've got to be kidding me. Where were you joined? I want to know!"

Carlo raised an eyebrow in question but Myrtle just waived the issue aside.

"Never mind, baby, now tell me your most favorite thing in the whole world, Carlo."

"I could say you, but you're too smart for that. A steak and a chilled bottle of good champagne. Are you mad?"

"No, I like it, baby, and I like you. I'm pondering where to take you for the best fucking steak in the whole world."

"Myrtle, we're not going to fuck, and you're not widowed, are you?"

"Correct, baby."

"Myrtle, about my equipment. I do not just make love, I impale."

"I know, baby, I've been checking you out. But as far as I'm concerned my Henry hung the moon, and I'd never cheat on him."

"Why did you and your friends come here tonight, Myrtle?"

"To fuck with you but not in that way."

"Just what I figured. Why can't I get a woman like you, Myrtle."

"You are a great natural resource, Carlo, and I think you should be married. I know lots of rich, lonely widows. I am going to marry your ass off, Carlo."

"Sounds good, Baby."
"How do you like your steak, Carlo?"
"Medium rare."
"Just what I figured," said Myrtle with a laugh.

BERTIE

Bertie was sitting at the kitchen table in his royal blue bath robe and corny Ronald Coleman slippers drinking coffee and eating cinnamon toast. Lavinia, also at the breakfast table, was drinking a V-8 Juice and popping aspirin. She was nursing a hangover after a night of rough sex.

Her gigilo, Bobby De Niro, had been more than accommodating taking her abuse in an upward fashion, very upward.

"Lavinia," said Bertie, "I've been thinking and maybe we should get a divorce. You've got your own money now and don't need me anymore."

"Oh, Bertie, no. You're a part of me and I do need you."

"I know it, baby, and you're a part of me, and always will be. I'll always love you."

"Oh, Bertie, we can work this out. I know we can. I never really meant to leave you. We can go to a marriage counselor. "

"No, baby, I'm sorry. I truly am. But you'll always be yourself. Who else can you be, baby?"

"Oh, Bertie, I'll change, turn over a new leaf."

"No, Lavinia, you won't. I'm Bertie, the lap dog, and I confess it excited me for a long time. I just need something, someone else different now."

"Oh, Bertie, no," and with that Lavinia got up and encircled his neck with her arms.

"It's too late, Lavinia. And honey, I'm taking the children. They'll be better off with me. Ever hear that Nat King Cole song, 'Ramblin' Rose'? 'How I loved her no one knows. Wild and wind blown,

That's how you've grown, No one can cling to a Ramblin' Rose.' That's us, baby."

"Oh, Bertie, I'm begging you, don't do this. I love you so."

"I know. I knew you better than you knew yourself. But, now I've got someone else, too. She's only a waitress but I think she can make me happy."

"Will she be true to you, Bertie?"

"Yes, Lavinia."

"Oh, Bertie, it hurts so bad. You're a part of me: you're my heart."

"I know, baby. And people thought I was a fool to love you. But I wasn't was I, my sweet girl."

"No, Bertie," she said and started to sob.

Bertie got up and put his arms around her patting her on the head with one large, gentle hand. Sometimes what is gentle can be more dangerous than that which is harsh and mean. Bertie just held her while she sobbed. It hurt her more than anything Armand ever did. Too late did she know her own heart. In a matter of time, she calmed down.

"All right, Bertie, I won't fight you about the children or anything else."

"Never thought you would, honey. And I'm going to give you a very generous settlement in case the book sales go south. You get your ass in a crack, and you just call old 'Uncle Bertie' and I'll get you out of the jam. Okay, honey? You're a good, sweet girl underneath. Nobody ever really knew you but me, Lavinia. My good, sweet girl. Now you go call Myrtle, baby. You can't be alone now."

"Oh, Bertie, Bertie," she screamed trying to hold him fast but he just gently disengaged himself and went out the door. Lavinia's heart was uprooted like a hapless weed. She never knew it that Bertie was her center, steadying her, and giving her the courage to be crass and mean, bitchy and bold. She was gutted like a carp. The things women don't know until it too late. Yes, the things. She called Myrtle in hysterics and went right over.

In the meantime another gentleman with the essence brimstone observed this scene, and he thought to himself, "She's too good for me but she's also as bad as I am. That bitch has got me in an uproar and I can't even zip up my goddamn pants! Why'd I even use His name! I'm immortal. What the fuck's going on? This is not supposed to be happening. I'm the fuck harvesting souls, and now this. Goddamnit!

His name again. She's bad but she's also very good not like Lady MacBeth or that poisoning bitch, Lucretia! I want to protect her, give her things, do the things a man should do, and I'm not even a man, so to speak. Except for the dick. His little joke on me. Can I make her love me? Luc, you don't know how to do this but you're sure going to try.

"You must have this woman! You must!"

Myrtle in the meantime looked at Lavinia in dismay. She had never seen her so upset and the liquor wasn't even helping. Who knew she really loved Bertie after all? Myrtle never would have guessed it. How could she? Myrtle, being a kind woman, was always ready to accept surfaces from people, taking them at face value. She never analyzed them. That was the devil's work she thought. Never pry and they'll never cry was her motto. She was afraid for Lavinia and surprised. And she sensed an unsettling male presence in the room and felt uneasy.

"Shit," she thought, "now I'm losing my mind, too. It's the both of us!"

"Oh, babes, they'll be another man for you. Please don't despair."

"They'll never be another Bertie, Myrtle. He was so good, and he wasn't weak at all. He was strong. Strong enough to love me! I was such a fool. Why didn't I know myself?"

"Who knows themselves, baby? I don't even know myself, and don't want to either. Something's sure giving me the creeps, Lavinia. I feel like we're being watched."

"Shit, Myrtle don't you go South, too. I need you to be tracking at this moment," replied Lavinia.

"Listen, honey, you don't worry about Old Myrt. It was a momentary lapse. We'll go to see Carlo. He's funnier than a motherfucker!"

"At this moment, I don't think Oedipus is all that amusing?"

"Who the fuck is Oedipus?" intoned Myrtle.

"No one. No, seriously, Myrt, who's Carlo?"

"The gigilo I met last night. He's a real piece of work. I'm going to marry him off to Rose Anne! She'll think he's the Second Coming while she's coming!"

"You're a matchmaker, now, Myrtle?"

"I am…many things. Lavinia."

"Myrt, I don't need dick right at this very moment."

"No, but you need to laugh, and I am calling him, bitch. So shut the fuck up. I know what I'm doing!"

So they called Carlo and he was glad to hear from Myrtle, his new friend. He invited them over to his apartment for brunch. After a while, they arrived at his center city high rise. It was late morning, and the sun was slanting sideways in the sky in a coy, you can't understand me, fashion.

Opening the door, still in his bathrobe, he greeted them with a kiss to each cheek and a light embrace. The scent of Calvin Klein's 'Obsession' wafted through the air. The apartment, decorated in black, white, and gray, resembled a spread in an elegant fashion magazine. The yellow roses, strategically placed, sighed and shivered in their long stemmed crystal vases. On the walls were big, bold, passionately colored erotic nudes.

"So, Myrtle, your friend has the broken heart. Now, you must go slow, pretty woman. Step softly in this life. You are an egg shell. Do not attempt any wars, or great undertakings now. You need softness, warmth, honeyed things, now. Do not use your power for evil out of bitterness and hurt. Be as weak as you need to be. You are safe here. Forgive yourself, and he who hurt you."

Lavinia crumbled and threw herself into his arms. He stood, holding her like a broken thing, and she cried and cried. "I know, baby. I know. Cry out your heart. Spit it on the floor if you need to. You shall heal in time, darling. You shall heal."

"Damn! Damn! Damn!" thought Luc, or Lucifer. "I must not let her fall in love with this jerk. Kind men are the bane of my existence! Kind men hurt women much more than I ever could. I love her! The damned bitch!"

Luc fumed and the room became over heated and Carlo noticed immediately telling Myrtle to open the windows. Myrtle thought,

"Carlo is a doll. If I weren't with Henry… My, oh my!"

Carlo directed them to sit on his plush black leather couch. On the side table a silver serving set bubbled with the aroma of fine Arabica coffee, and whole fresh cream floated placidly in an elegant urn. A small antique container held sugar cubes. Glancing over on the kitchen table they saw a huge cut crystal bowl of melons, bananas, strawberries and green grapes, and a basket of assorted muffins, both light and dark.

"When we are through talking, ladies, we will adjourn to the kitchen where I will make you my special omelet. A little known fact is I used to be an executive chef at a five star hotel. You are in for a treat, and also we will have chilled mimosas. Tell me of your heart, beautiful one. Myrtle, you may talk, too."

"No, babes, this is Lavinia's show. Besides all I ever talk about is the grocery list and my ability to iron men's shirts. As for me, if it aint broke, don't fix it!" And she laughed, a crude, rambunctious laugh, the only way Myrtle knew how to do it.

"I love your laugh, baby," he said.

"I cannot find my heart," interjected Lavinia. "It just feels blank."

"That's because you are ill inside, baby. It will be that way for a time. I know the pain you feel." And he had an impulse to reach out and lay a comforting hand on her head but something checked him. Something or someone.

Then Lavinia told him her story, all of it, and how she mistreated Bertie for years. Carlo did not judge, and only listened. When she had exhausted herself he began to speak.

"One in the hand is worth two in the bush as you Americans say. Poor baby, you didn't know. How little we really know ourselves. We do not know. We are human: we make mistakes. Is there a chance for reconciliation?"

Lavinia shook her head, crying all the more. "No, Carlo, he meant it. Every word. I know Bertie."

"Cry, baby, cry. Someday it will be a memory, the pain, like smoke from a campfire. It will become hazy, distant to you. The heart is elastic. It can stretch over the Grand Canyon, and back. Believe me. I know this if I know anything. Now, I want you two ladies to have a laugh. Come into Carlo's 'Palace of Pussy.'"

He led them into his bed room and on the walls were women's torsos in charcoal in every stage of arousal, mountains of breasts, and giant gaping holes, and bodacious asses. Both Myrtle and Lavinia burst out into gales of laughter. It was outrageous. It was lewd. It was marvelous.

"Where in the hell did you get these things, Carlo?" asked Myrtle.

"It's my work, and those in the living room, too," he replied. "I love woman as you can see. They are the great solace in my life. Woman and food. I am not a greatly educated man, but I do know art."

"And how to produce it," said Lavinia.

"Say, I've just had an idea," he said. "Lavinia, you will be my model. I always worked from memory before. I love your ivory skin, and long, shapely body. You remind me of a Modigliani."

"Really?" said Lavinia, her mood lifting a bit.

"The sound of the pencil scratching on paper. The stillness in the air. The completed creations. These things will heal you. And I will get you drunk on wine and food. There will be no cock. Cock is what broke you heart. I will admire you from a far like a goddess. The goddess that you are."

"You'd do that for me?" asked Lavinia.

"You're Myrtle's friend. That's all I need. I am the Doctor of Broken Hearts."

"Then I guess I'll learn how the Duchess of Alba felt. Why the fuck not? What do you think, Myrt?"

"I think it sounds great. And Carlo, you already know how I'll thank you."

"Excuse me?" replied Lavinia archly.

"Not that, asshole. I'm going to find him a rich wife. Rose Anne looks good," replied Myrtle.

"Rose Anne! She's a cow, barely literate!" brayed Lavinia.

"True, she's no literary light. But she's still young and she's smart about life, dear. And rich as hell. And she has kids and can have more."

Carlo wants children, don't you, Carlo?"

"Yes, Myrtle. How did you know?"

"You're Italian, aint you?" she replied.

"And why not me? I'm rich, too, and available," said Lavinia.

"You're a bitch, babes. Carlo needs another kind of a woman. And besides, he told you no cock, didn't he?"

"Why not me, Carlo?" asked Lavinia.

"I find myself afraid for some reason. I do not really know, Lavinia. I have a difficult feeling in my heart like you're not meant to be my woman, and I don't know where it is coming from."

"Oh, what the hell. You're right. I really don't need dick. It's the last thing I need, You're a smart man, Carlo."

Luc smiled from the far corner of the room, unseen and powerful, and he thought, "Better smart than dead, gigilo." He then lifted his hand from Carlo's cock.

LUC OBSERVES

In the months that followed Luc observed the interaction between Carlo and Lavinia watching for erotic signals that might pass between them. Every time he sensed a situation arising, (and that is the right word), he quelled it. Every time Carlo felt the least bit of desire Luc reached into his pants and constricted his cock. It felt like numerous, painful, tight bands going around it and Carlo felt alarmed and went to a doctor who found nothing.

Carlo then thought, "She's an evil bitch and that's why." But how on the other hand could an evil person quote Emily Dickinson, 'The wounded dear leaps highest'? And how could she be so personable and witty and warm? He wondered about his own virility for the first time in his life. But with Rose Anne this was not the case. He was all over her resplendent, white flesh like a Viking invader.

"Carlo," she asked one day, "what was your best piece of ass?"

"Best piece of ass? Well that would have to be Barbara June, six feet of platinum blond from Texas with an ass so large I could not get my hands around it." He spread out the fingers of both gigantic hands for emphasis.

"She kept me up for two days. Oh, we slept a bit for a few hours then she would wake me up in one way or another. And those lips, so thick and shapely, good for what you can imagine! And she smelled like sunflowers, the earth. There was a snap in her back like the tip of a whip: it was a wind up and release like the great ebb and flow of tides. I never have known a woman so strong and passionate. And rich and generous, so very rich. Her husband was an oil baron. But, I was glad to see her go. Too much of a good thing, you know."

"And your worst piece?" Lavinia asked.

"You're just like Myrtle. So curious. What are you doing making a damn graph of my exploits?"

"I'm a writer, silly. I may make you the hero of my next book."

"Then you have no sense of what a hero is. And what would be the title?"

"I thought of calling it 'Eros' but my readers probably wouldn't understand the word."

"And you think I do?"

"Yep! And back to it, your worst piece?"

"You are a persistent one, dear."

"Spill it, Carlo."

"My worst piece. And you would expect me to say an old women who smelled and had false teeth, wouldn't you? Actually, it was a beautiful, young girl with absolutely no aptitude for making love and graceless as a toad! She kept asking me did I "love" her, was she pretty, would I die for her? I suspect she was a bit ill, and for sure, she was frigid. She put more trust in a word than in what I was trying to give her. Sex is giving, and it is not a word as is love. Love is of the spirit and the spirit has no words. Young girls often make that mistake. They think if you say you love them that you must. The truth is in what a man does, and not in what he says. Some women never grow out of this. They crave the word, and worship lies."

"And what words do you have for me, Carlo?"

"Lovely, and dangerous, baby."

"And you can tell that?"

"It's in your eyes. It's in your scent. It's not so much in what you say."

"Are you afraid of me, Carlo?"

"I think, you have dangerous curves, darling."

"What is it really?"

"Something. I don't really know why, baby. Some instinct just tells me to stay away from you."

"Do you think I'm a maniac? Is that it?"

"Definitely not. You are not crazy. No, not crazy. It's something else. I can't put my finger on it. When I get too near you it's like I feel a hand constricting my heart, and my balls, for that matter."

"Explain that to me."

"I have, baby, I have. I can't explain it any better. Besides Rose Anne is my woman now. I will marry her if I have my way. She's a good woman."

"Damn. And the pictures you draw of me are so…frank."

"Sublimation is the better part of art, and discretion is the better part of valor."

"And I thought you were not an educated man, Carlo."

"And, I am not, Lavinia. It's just that I learn from and listen to my clients. Turn on your back now, my girl. I must catch the long slant of your elegant back into the plush curve of your ass."

Lavinia did as told. She could not understand Carlo but she knew he was resolute. She relaxed and it was as if she did not exist as a mind at all. She was the tip of his graffite pencil as it traveled across the page, and she was content. Content to be an artist's muse. The still air enfolded her, and Carlo's eyes looked like two pools of liquid obsidian.

The months wore on and Carlo held her warm in the pearlescent shell of his simple, manly friendship and she began to heal just as he said she would. He shielded her from poisonous thoughts and loneliness and he gave her entire days. At night he practiced his craft and sometimes he went to see his "beloved" Rose Anne as Lavinia thought of her. She knew it was of no use so she did not try any more to seduce him. Being a muse was entirely satisfactory, and this did surprise her.

This did not surprise Carlo that she did not contradict him. He knew his own power and believed in his own goodness. And he was right to do so. "Never break a woman on the anvil of cock." This is what he thought but not in those exact words.

After about six months, she began to feel much better and started to look at men with the old hunger and yearning in her eyes. It was the Friday before Thanksgiving and she was in an upscale market buying her produce for the week. She was buying strawberries, tomatoes, bananas, and peaches. As her hand reached out to select her peaches she felt an overwhelming male presence. Someone was staring hard at her ass and backside. She looked abruptly to the left of her and was met by a pair of bold, yellow eyes. His gaze sent from the peach in her hand, to her small, tight breasts then to her eyes.

And he said, in a low, melodious voice, "Nice peaches, aren't they?"

She burst out in laughter, and said, "And aren't you the fresh one!"

"Si," he replied.

"Are you Italian?"

"No, but in my business one gets to know many, many Italians. Are you clairvoyant, miss?"

"Maybe," she replied.

"Then you must know I intend to take you out to the best goddamn dinner you ever had in your whole life! Your name, please."

"Lavinia, and yours?"

"The name's Luc, and I am astounded to meet you!"

Lavina thought, "Damn, he's beautiful. Just like a fucking fallen angel." And, of course, he was both. His lower face had that bluish tinge of a man with a heavy beard. "Such testosterone!" A look of hunger and lust infused his face yet it was an intelligent face with close set, piercing amber eyes surrounded by lush black lashes. She noted his full, cruelly beautiful, red mouth and high, sculpted cheek bones with a double cleft in his chin. It was a rugged face right out of Italian Vogue. She glanced quickly between his legs and he caught her and laughed, saying nothing. And he smelled like bitter cloves.

"Will you come out with me, Lavinia? I promise I won't bite... unless you like that sort of thing. I'm your neighbor, and live right down the block. I've noticed you many times but you've never noticed me. In fact, I've seen you so often I almost feel as if I know you already!"

And he lightly touched her wrist and she felt her arm infuse with a curious warmth.

"Well, I just got out of a marriage..."

"Please, please, Lavinia. I have all your books. I confess I know your name, and hope you will consent to know me. This is very important to me, Lavinia. We'll meet in public, and I'll tell you anything you want to know about me. Give you my family tree is you so desire."

He was so earnest, so passionate that she laughed out loud. It was absurd. It was marvelous. After accepting his invitation, she thought to herself, "And it's about time, bitch."

GOODBYE, DEAR HENRY

Myrtle dreamed she was in a garden in a long, white, Victorian gown standing on wet cobblestones, and there were all these dead crows lying on the pavement in a triangle with the apex pointing to her. There must have been about seventy of them with rivulets of red blood streaming from their ghastly dead beaks. And for some reason she could sense their dead eyes like hard, yellow pieces of glass, staring up at the gray, rain-flecked sky. And in her dream she knew they came for her Henry, and she woke up screaming.

He died doing what he did best, fucking his blond, young secretary. The girl, named Lucy, had called Myrtle the previous afternoon in hysterics and she had told Myrtle the circumstances of Henry's death. When she heard this, Myrtle let out a wild, raucous laugh and she said, "Don't worry, dear. At least he died doing what he was best at. Henry was the King of Fuck!"

Then she hung up the phone, doubled over in pain, and screamed and screamed. Then she got the butcher knife from the kitchen, going back into the living room, to stab her couches over and over again with the blade. She was not mad at the infidelity: she was mad at God for taking Henry too soon in the prime of his life. Then she got a bottle of scotch and went to bed, and thought, "Tonight, I fall apart. Tomorrow, I deal." The phone rang and rang but she did not answer.

The following morning she awoke to the insistent ringing of her door bell and thought, "It's probably the police. The girls, no doubt, think I've offed myself which is quite a meritorious thought. But how? Hang myself with my own lace panties and make some really first class yellow journalism. Like they'd hold up my fat ass. Poisoning is out: don't like pills. I know, a slow death by liquor, have fun while offing myself, Now there's the ticket!"

"Who the fuck is bugging me at six o'clock in the morning? Jack asses! No respect for the widow!"

She opened the door to her two friends, Gladys and Lavinia.

"Since you hadn't answered your phone all day yesterday we were going to axe your door. We heard the news about Henry!" said Gladys.

Myrtle took one look at the maniacal look in Gladys' eyes and burst out laughing.

"Well, fuck it bitch. You should see yourself from this end. You think you're goddamned Paul Bunyan or something?"

"What the hell were you doing to worry us like this, Myrtle?" fumed Lavinia.

Myrtle said nothing and simply went over and breathed into Lavinia's face.

"Holy shit! Instead of 'A Star is Born' it's An Alcoholic is Born," quipped Lavinia.

"You scared the shit out of us, bitch. We're fucking getting a contact drunk."

"Well, quit your worrying. I'm okay," said Myrtle.

"You are not okay!", they both intoned.

"No, I'm not. What am I going to do without my Henry? What?"

And she began to cry beating her fists against her thighs. Lavinia then pinned her arms behind her.

"Carlo, is worried too, Myrtle. He's the one who gave us the axe," said Lavinia.

"Well, it's nice to have friends. All of you."

"Bertie says he can get you a deal on the funeral, casket, plot and the like. Even though, we're not together he still wants to help," said Lavinia.

"Clive and I will do anything we can. You know that, dear. And Enrique says he'll do all the floral arrangements free. He still calls you 'la Gordita' since he hasn't seen you in so long," piped in Gladys.

"Well, thanks to all of you. But I've already got something planned. A grand blow out, an ultra wake, with live band, belly dancers, catered food, and lots and lots of drinking. Henry liked a good party when he was alive: there's no need to think that has changed. I'm inviting every person Henry ever knew including his paramours. Anyone who ever knew and loved my Henry.

Ashes to ashes,

Dust to dust,

Wish you were here to feel my bust!"

Oh, Henry, Henry." And she began to cry big, merciless, leaden tears torn from her heart.

After she had calmed down a bit and was sitting in her kitchen, Lavinia spoke,

"Myrtle, I've got something totally inappropriate and outrageous to tell you. On the news, I just heard David Duchovny, the star of the old X Files is a sex addict. Now, I ask you why couldn't it have been Johnny Depp?"

Myrtle nearly busted a gut, as the saying goes. "There's no justice, dear."

"On the serious side, when's the funeral?" asked Lavinia.

"Friday, a week. Friday was his favorite day. Said you could get more pussy on Friday than any other day of the week. It's going to be at St. Peters."

"But, Myrt, you're not Catholic. Neither was Henry," said Gladys.

"But they have the nicest churches and I told the priest I was."

"Listen, bitch, if you want to be 'Catholic for a Day' I have no objections," said Lavinia.

"Me either," said Gladys and embraced her. "What can we do for you right now, honey?"

"Stay with me the week and get me some brie and Carr's crackers. I'm hungry as shit."

"Sure we will," said Lavinia. "Who've I got after all, me, myself and I. Although there's this new guy named Luc."

"Are you sure you're ready, honey? You're still getting over Bertie and then there was Armand," said Myrtle.

"Honey, this little fledgling can fly her ass off. Let's worry about you now, Myrt," she replied.

"Please, please, honey. This is all about you," intoned Gladys.

"Just do me one favor, girls. Make sure I'm sober for the funeral."

"Consider it done, baby," said Lavinia.

And the three made it through the week in total solidarity.

At the funeral, people came in droves and packed the church. Henry knew the whole world it seemed, and no eye was dry during the service.

Myrtle wondered how many lovers were present and she welcomed them all in her big, big heart. The priest's face took on the aspect of melting paraffin in the candle light, and his words, kind and true echoed throughout the cathedral. She felt the presence of Henry's large, happy spirit during the sermon and let the tears flow.

After he had said his last prayers, Myrtle took the podium and said in a steady clear voice, "I thank you all for coming, employees, friends, and in some cases, lovers. My Henry was a man who loved often and loved well. And that, my friends, was the beauty of Henry. He was too large for just one person. My address is on the announcements and I invite you all, friends and lovers alike, to my home for a big party. On your way out at the receiving line I ask you to tell me who you are and what you meant to my Henry. All are welcome in my heart."

Toward the end a man came up to Myrtle and identified himself as an associate of Henry's, his lover. Myrtle's mouth flew open, and then she slapped him on the back, saying, "What the hell, Henry. Never a dull moment!" And she planted a big kiss on his cheek and told him he was riding with her to the party to which he replied that he wouldn't have it any other way. She asked if his name was Kevin or Brian and he told her, "Kevin."

"What the hell, honey, we all have our crosses to bear. Did your mother cause you to be gay by giving you that name?"

Oh, hell, yes," he replied and then said, "Mrs. Sullivan you were the only one who had his heart and I can sure see why."

"Apparently, Henry never met a man he didn't like."

"No, that's not true, Mrs. Sullivan. I was his only man. For once in my life, I got lucky. But you were his end all and be all, believe me."

"Well, honey, aren't you sweet."

"No, I'm a bitch," he replied.

"Then we'll get on famously. Call me Myrtle, babe."

The party was outrageous. People got roaring drunk, paired off, and lost all semblance of common sense. It was truly a "Henry" party.

Afterward, Myrtle walked through the house clearing up party refuse and checking for unwanted night guests. When she found them she politely and firmly asked them to leave. After the girls had gone to their respective homes she felt the presence of his smile engulfing her like a fine mist, and his warm, manly love burned in her heart.

She awoke much later huddled up in the fetal position on their huge, queen sized bed and she reached for the bottle and did not stop drinking the rest of the night. Then it was endless, jagged sorrow and the sky rained down hail and thunder. She stood at the window letting the rain drench her and she thought, "See, he is telling me he misses me, too."

In the days and weeks that followed she didn't stop drinking: she was trying to quit this earth, and it wasn't fun as she had told herself it would be. Endless, empty days followed like a chain of paper clips linked together in a hellish infinity. The girls were alarmed and made a decision to have her committed as she would not see them nor return their calls. They realized she was drinking herself into oblivion and possibly death.

The day before they had arranged for her commitment, they ran into Kevin, Henry's lover, and told him of her plight. He was aghast and shocked and firmly told them that he would take matters into his hands as he had much experience in matters of this kind. They were convinced by his harsh and forceful entreaty and they arranged to wait a few days on the commitment.

The next day, Kevin and two very large female impersonators, one black, and one white, rang her door bell and did not stop. When she finally opened the door in a drunken haze, Kevin said simply, "Myrtle, honey, we're here to help. Let us the fuck in, baby."

From her eyes it looked like Felini's Satyricon if she would have seen the movie. Kevin, attired in a Ralph Lauren shirt, khaki pants, and loafers looked the picture of propriety. The queens, having come from their club, were attired in outrageous, glittering gowns resplendent with ostrich feathers, and exotic furs. Miss Liz, the white one, looked like her name sake in exact detail right down to the violet eyes, and porcelain skin, and in heels she stood about six feet one. Her compatriot, Miss Eartha, looked incredibly like that chanteuse of old with her high cheek bones, snapping brown eyes, and wiry frame. They smelled of expensive perfume, perhaps Chanel, or so Myrtle thought, and they flounced on in the front door like they owned the place. No proper queen can be without "attitude".

"Darling, you look as if you've seen a ghost, and not Henry's ghost. We're here to get you squared away. You need help," said Kevin who introduced the other two, using their stage names.

"Haven't you ever seen a queen, before, doll?" asked Miss Eartha.

"Can't rightly say that I have," Myrtle replied with a small laugh.

"She laughed, Kev, it's a good sign!" said Miss Liz.

"Darling, we're going to get you all cleaned up, put you in the shower, and make you a nice breakfast. Eartha, you take her upstairs. Liz and I'll get breakfast," commanded Kevin.

On the way up to the shower, Miss Eartha felt compelled to give her some advice. "Listen, doll, a lady should be always dainty about her person, smell good and all. Even after the act of love. Good, I like this. You've got deodorant and plenty of perfume. This'll do nicely, honey."

Miss Eartha put her in the shower admonishing her to "wash that pussy" and other visceral suggestions, and Myrtle just laughed her ass off. Afterward, Miss Eartha dried off her back and handed her a clean bathrobe hanging on the hook.

"See, doll, good as new. Old Auntie Eartha knows what she's doing. Let's go downstairs and get some grub."

When she got below Miss Liz was frying up the eggs, and Kevin was doing everything else.

"What's the matter, sweetie? Haven't you ever seen a queen frying an egg?" asked Miss Liz.

"A resounding no to that one," she replied.

"Well, get used to it. We're your new sisters until you get well. We'll be staying over, doll," said Miss Liz.

"We're going to feed your ass, honey. Then we talk. It's kind of going to be like the Camp Fire Girls," intoned Kevin. "You smell like a fucking, angel, Myrtle. I hoped we're not too much of a shock to your nervous system. Your girls told me you were in a jam, and ask yourself, honey, would Henry want to see you like this? Think on that. Now eat your eggs, baby, and drink plenty of coffee. Black preferably."

"This is very sweet of you, Kevin."

"Sweet, nothing. I just don't want Henry's ghost kicking my damn ass!" and he laughed.

"I guess he wouldn't be too pleased," said Myrtle.

"Damn straight. And Liz and Eartha want you to know they both have all their original equipment if you're wondering."

"That's just wonderful, dear" replied Myrtle.

"You have no idea, my dear," said Miss Liz rolling her violet eyes.

"Darling, you look practically anemic," said Miss Eartha. "I'm going to call my mom and get her hush puppy recipe and the one for black eyed peas. You need some soul food,"

"Soul food is great," replied Myrtle.

"Darling, I don't recall you being so damn conciliatory," said Kevin.

"Don't know my ass from a hole in the ground anymore," replied Myrtle.

Miss Liz got up from her seat with a look of mirth on her face and went and whispered in Myrtle's ear. "Honey, it's the one with the hair around the outside."

Myrtle blasted the room with her laughter, and said, "Well, thank you, dear."

"That's more like it, Myrtle. Women are just tits and battery acid," said Kevin.

"Not this woman, Kevin."

"I was just generalizing. No, not you, Myrtle. Definitely not. You're more like a peach, a big, fat juicy peach. We're going to help you get your sassy back," said Kevin.

"What the hell for. I'll never get a man like Henry again,"

"Nor will I but life goes on. You've got to believe that, hon."

"I don't want to even try. I used to be the life of the party but no more. I can't go on without him, Kevin."

"Myrtle," he said, "I detect a serious note of self pity, and that's not like you."

Miss Liz drew herself up to her full six feet two, and said, "Imagine my dismay as a youngster to find I wasn't a girl. Trying mommy's clothes on is just not a happening thing in the deep South. They like their Scarlet O'Hara's to have pussies down there."

"And what the hell happened to your couches, Myrtle," asked Miss Eartha.

"They had an accident."

"Well, get new ones, today," commanded Kevin. "Where are we supposed to park our asses since we're staying over with you?"

"Yeah, doll, interjected Miss Eartha, "we're not girl scouts at a fucking pledge meeting! We can't sit on the floor."

"Darling," said Miss Eartha, "you're rich. Why not get yourself a couple of gigolo's to fuck the shit out of you. It is what ails you, babe."

"I don't want any man or anyone else for that matter," snapped Myrtle.

"So you want to die, is that it? Listen, Myrtle, I'm bipolar and I want to die every other day. The world's a shit hole, Myrtle, and we've got to make it beautiful," said Kevin.

"You can't go on doing this, darling," said Miss Liz. "The house smells like a cat box and you didn't even have any food in the fridge. We had to go out and buy it. Not that we minded."

"We're going to put you back together. Get used to it, hon," said Kevin.

Myrtle burst into tears at their kindness.

The two queens burst into a dramatic rendition of the song, 'Cry me a River.'

"Now you say you love me and just to prove it's true,
I want you to cry me a river, cry me a river,
Because I cried a river over you."

And then Myrtle laughed her loud, raucous laugh. In fact, she laughed her ass off..almost.

"Darling," said Miss Eartha on a serious note, "I had a man who died last September, and I went all to pieces just like you. Well, not exactly just like you. I shot meth, drank a bottle of Dewar's a day, and fucked any body who looked my way. I was for sure trying to kill myself. I went totally out of my head. And Kevin, wait until you hear what that fucker did. One day he handed me a loaded pistol, and said, 'Here do it right, bitch. You're inefficient'. I hauled off and popped him a good one. And he got up, brushed himself off, and said, 'Kick my ass all you want. But what's it going to be. Live or die? Make up your fucking mind.' And now, I say the same to you, Myrtle."

"We've all had someone we loved die on us, Myrtle. We're gay and aids is rampant. You just can't fall apart. Do you think your Henry would want this for you, Myrtle?" asked Miss Liz.

"She's right, Myrtle. You're a strong woman and Henry would be very displeased with you right now. You fake it until you make it, hon," said Kevin.

"I guess I could try."

"Damn straight you will try. A pill doctor and some grief counseling are what we're going to do with you. Fuck it all. You Will Survive."

"Darling, we need some work clothes to clean this fucking house. How about Henry's closet, or better yet, your closet. You got something to fit us, babe?" said Miss Liz.

"I could call my old servant, Mauve."

"No one cleans like a gay man, hon. Why eat chuck when you've got steak?" said Kevin.

"Take us to your closet. I've got to get out of this gown and these fucking stilettos." said Miss Liz.

"You got anything in tangerine? That's my color," said Miss Eartha.

"Come along, girls, I used to be a lot bigger than I am now, and I've got plenty that will fit you."

Upon seeing Myrtle's designs, both queens shrieked in delight.

"Will, you look at these clothes, Liz. A faux leopard skin sheath with matching pill box hat! Where'd you get these marvelous clothes, girl?"

"Yes, where?" intoned Miss Liz. "I love the pink chiffon evening dress with the feathers. It's just precious, darling! This definitely aint Macy's or Nieman Marcus!"

"Well, girls, I design these clothes myself. I can't find what I want in the stores."

"Oh, doll, you are so talented," said Miss Eartha.

"Yes, talented," echoed Miss Liz. "May I wear the turquoise pants suit? It's so Grace Kelly or Jackie O."

"Definitely, Jackie O." said Miss Eartha. "Girl, you know Gracie never fucked with pants suits. Liz, you know that!"

"So, I made a mistake. I was excited," came her reply.

"I'll wear the tangerine slacks and halter top. I'll look far better than you, bitch," she said to Miss Liz.

"Well, fuck off, cunt. Oops, that's right, you don't have one," said Miss Liz.

"You either," came the reply.

"Wear anything you want, girls. I can't wear them anymore. In fact, take anything you want from my entire closet," said Myrtle.

"Oh, shit, I've died and gone to fashion heaven," said Miss Liz.

"Me fucking too," replied Miss Eartha.

"Say, Myrt, are you bored with being just a housewife. That is, when you do it?" asked Miss Liz.

"I never gave it much thought."

"Well, give it a thought. You could make a shit load of money with these designs selling to people such as us."

"Oh, no. I'm not good enough to be professional and I've never worked my entire life."

"What do you mean not professional. Eartha, have you ever in your life seen such a seam. You do your own sewing, don't you, Myrtle?"

"Sure, but I don't need the money."

"Well, we, as your friends, need the money," said Miss Liz.

"Art transcends life. Think on that, darling," said Miss Eartha. "Let's get Kevin."

"Yes, let's."

Kevin came in and fell out when he saw her designs.

"Listen, Myrtle. I've got a degree from Wharton and I've got contacts in the fashion industry. You know, stores, designers, bankers. We, as a people, need our own designer. Will you please consider it when you're better? It's Big Business, Myrtle."

"I think I feel a good bit better now. Still sad, but not so sad."

"Here, drink this Virgin Mary. Vitamin C and work could play a very large role in you total recovery. Work will get you to take your mind off yourself, and your loss. Granted it was a great loss but I lost him, too, hon," said Kevin.

"Remember us, your friends. A friend in need is a friend, indeed," said Miss Liz.

"Well, girls and Kevin, I might do it."

"No, might about it, hon. Do it or we'll fuck you. A straight woman being fucked by three gay men. Not a pretty sight, my dear," said Kevin.

"Could you?" asked Myrtle coyly.

"We can fuck cats if we want," replied Miss Liz, and she laughed.

"I'm thinking it's the right thing to do," replied Myrtle.

"Well, all right, bitch," said Kevin and all three of them hugged her at once tightly.

And Myrtle thought to herself as they pressed into her, "So gays are really hung, too. Where are all those small dick wonders in the world women complain about? I sure haven't met any!"

THE PRINCE OF DARKNESS

"You don't say? And he just jumped up and ran out for no reason? That's terrible. Just terrible," said Luc, his head cocked to the side in a sympathetic manner. He was sitting across from Lavinia at a very expensive, candelabra and linen, restaurant. It was his restaurant, Il Diablo.

"Yes, I liked him very much, and we were in bed. It was one of those things, you know like the poem that goes, 'Only God can love you for yourself alone and not your yellow hair'. He was Irish and his name was Seamus which is Irish for James, and he had this outrageous red, auburn hair. It practically cast a tint on the walls of the bar. Anyway he goes inside me, and then pulls out and says 'Woman ye are cold as ice. Are ye a succubus? A wife of the devil?' And he just ran from the room. Didn't even have his clothes on all the way. I am so upset. I'm going to the GYN right away!"

"Well, girl, that wouldn't have happened with me: I can assure you. A wife of the devil. That's very interesting. So, poetic, the Irish." And he made a mental note to give all red haired people lots of freckles, big, orange, ugly freckles.

"Fact, is, you should have been with me instead and that's the solution. Be with me!" And he put a sympathetic hand on the inside of her wrist and she felt the familiar warm sensation.

"

I am so upset. He meant it about me being a succubus!" she said close to tears.

"Well, that's not always an insult. Like if I said it." And he laughed.

She noted the whiteness of his teeth, and their seeming sharpness and felt a chill. There was something very feral about him, and his eyes alarmed, repelled, and attracted her. So amber were they and so intense. She surmised serial killers would have those kinds of eyes yet he was so sympathetic and "warm". As if noting her thought, he softened his expression into that of a puppy dog begging for table scraps.

Lavinia relaxed, and said, "One other man called me that but he was just being ironic."

"I suspect you could never even hurt a fly, Lavinia," he said.

"Damn!", thought Lavinia. "He knows, but how does her know?"

"Tell me about yourself, Luc."

"All right. I'm a businessman but how original is that? Every man always says that even if he's a file clerk! I have dealings with Italians, Sicilians, actually, as you would probably surmise from my earlier conversation, and I own restaurants, and some publishing houses. Noir Publishing is one of my imprints. We do prose and poetry but no non-fiction. I hate the facts. 'Just the facts, ma'am.' Remember Sergeant Joe Friday off the old 'Dragnet' series? Well, I like creativity, the imagination. If I want facts, I read the damn newspaper. We like things in the nature of what you do, Lavinia."

"You're Noir Publishing? Wow! That's, as big as Curtis Brown, Harcourt Brace, and Random House. I'm impressed, Luc."

"I was rather hoping so. I could get you a better book deal like seventy/thirty."

"Wow! That's unheard of! And what would you want in return?"

Luc leaned forward and took her hand, and said, "Think on it, my dear."

"Oh," said Lavina who blushed hot pink.

"Darling," said Luc, "I suggest the oysters on the half shell purely for the reason that I want to see you eat them, and the filet mignon, rare, with pasta and cold asparagus spears. Our pasta is excellent here and homemade. In fact, the woman who makes it looks like the lady on the Contadina tomato paste can, and the goddamn chef looks like Fatty Arbuckle. Of course, without the killer instinct."

"And do you have a killer instinct, Luc?"

"Don't need one, darling. I have everything I need except for one thing."

"What is the one thing?" asked Lavinia.

"I decline to say at the moment. It may be a Sunday subscription to the New York Times, however. You're still wondering about me, I can see that. What do you want to know?"

"How old are you, Luc?"

"As old as Genesis, my dear."

"No, really how old are you, Luc."

"Well, how old are you, Lavinia?"

"Forty-three."

"That's how old I am, give or take a year or two."

"And where did you come from and tell me about your family, brothers and sisters, and the like."

"I come from where it's very hot out west, Texas, maybe, and I am the black sheep of my family. My brothers and sisters were all angels compared to me. My father said I was vain, no good, and threw me out of the pearly gates, so to speak. He hates me, that is if he were the hating kind."

"And does he hate you, Luc?"

"I would say we are at opposite ends of the table. Maybe hate is too strong a word. Some say he is a wonderful man. I just can't see that in particular. I think him impractical, an idealist. I go for the things of this world: he cares for spiritual things only. Never the twain shall meet."

"That's sad, Luc."

"You can never go home again, baby. And, as they say, water under the bridge. I don't give a shit."

"May I see a picture of you, and your family, Luc?"

"No, babe, they were all killed in a plane crash some years ago, and it's too painful to look at the photos for me. But my father survived. He survives all things."

"And you're not Italian?"

"Serbian, baby. We're a dark race."

"Were you ever married, Luc?"

"Never wanted to until now," he replied.

Lavinia dropped her fork and when she went to pick it up Luc was already placing it in her hand.

"Don't use that fork. But, of course, you know that. Even in good restaurants like mine, there are bugs. They say God never makes a mistake but I beg to differ. What useful purpose do cockroaches serve?

Futhermore, one of the Ten Commandments is 'Thou Shalt Not Kill' and how many armies did God send armies to 'smite' the enemies of the Israelites. It's hypocritical!"

"Luc, about what you said before. You barely know me. How can you speak of marriage, or is that just a line?"

"First off, I know you better than you think, better than you'll ever realize, and, yes, I am serious. I don't joke about such things."

"I think," said Lavinia, getting up abruptly, "I'd better go home."

"Wait, Lavinia," he said, getting up as well. "I cannot let you leave like this, darling. We, Serbs, are a passionate people who exaggerate all the time. I meant it when I said it, and now I see you're absolutely right. I can't help it. I really really like you. I want to know you and make you happy. What's so wrong about that? Please sit back down, baby."

"Well, I'm not used to all this passion,"

"Get used to it, baby. You and I are going places. Here's a man who is going to hand you the world on a silver platter. Think you're rich, now? Babe, it's a pittance compared to what you will have. You just wait and see, honey."

"Luc, what do you really want out of all this?, she asked.

"I think it best not to say for now. Let's take it slow, okay? I've got a great evening planned. Later on we're going to a private screening of 'The Seventh Seal' and then on to Manhattan for a party.

"Is that the movie where the main character plays chess with Death in an attempt to delay or avoid his own demise?"

"That's the one. And who's to say Death isn't just like that. Why's he always portrayed as a skeleton with a scythe. Maybe he's got a droll sense of humor, and dances, or something."

"You talk about it as if he were a real person, Luc."

"Of course, death is not a person. It's fiction, a movie, and I love movies, particularly Bergman films."

"I bet you love a lot of things, Luc. What are they?"

"Raindrops and roses and warm, yellow mittens, snowflakes that stay on my nose and eyelashes. These are a few of my favorite things! Let's hear about you, lady."

"You say you already know."

"Sure, but I don't know the little nuances. Your favorite author, artist, color, food," asked Luc.

"All right. Flannery O'Connor, Egon Schiele, pink and green, and avocadoes.

You."

"Lavinia, Lavinia, and Lavinia. Give me your hand and I'll show you my other favorite thing." He stuck her hand in his pants revealing an immense density and hardness.

"You are fresh, Luc," she said retrieving her hand.

"No, merely alive, my lovely. Waiter, check, please."

When they arrived later on in Manhattan at the party Lavinia asked Luc who was at the party, and he told her his associates and favorite people. She evinced the theory that Italians were God's people and a look of mirth appeared on his face and he replied, "Not hardly, my love."

At the party Lavinia saw the "old world" gentleman who helped her with the birth control situation. He and his "associates" had bailed Bertie out of extreme financial difficulties becoming his "silent partners".

"Yo! Miss 'Vinia heard you were big time now with all the books. The wife loves your work. What are you doing with "The Boss"?

"But, Vito, he not Sicilian!"

"No, hon, he's not. I better not say nothing. Mangia, mangia. You're skinny as shit. Don't tell him we talked."

Everywhere she looked were beautiful, shimmering, raven haired people. Luc had told her to circulate as he had business to attend to. She looked at the white marble columns, green marble dance floor, and antique walnut bar and tables. Glasses clinked together and laughter hummed throughout the room. Old disco tunes, such as 'I Will Survive' throbbed through the loud sound system. And she thought, "These people are just like me" and didn't know why she thought that. Numerous men, redolent of olive oil, and Campari, held her gaze with their hot black eyes and some boldly slapped her on the ass as she made her way to the buffet table. She felt a pulse between her legs and a pleasure that is also partly pain.

A jagged ice sculpture of a dying swan dominated the buffet table and in the cracked ice around it were lobster tails, Dungeness crabs, shrimp, and oysters and clams on the half shell. The hot table and desert table were equally grand. Mostly she noted the tall red, green, yellow and violet colored liquers glowing in their respective bottles. Two women stood at the buffet. One was a tall blond who had the look of a woman who had known too much of raw, dirty sex. Her companion, a daughter of Sicily, thin and elegant, was sucking on her tit, and caressing her vacant, lovely face. Their sheaths glowed gold and silver in the dark light of the room and the men watched hungrily. A husk of thick, expensive perfume permeated the air and mixed the dog raw scent of sex.

"Watch it," said Luc, coming up from behind her, placing a possessive hand on her ass, "These are the real succubuses!" and he laughed his low laugh which was somewhat like a growl. An electric spark shot up her ass to her spine and she gasped. He turned her around and tongued her in the mouth, pressing his body hard into her. The taste of his mouth was hot like Mexican peppers, and she was thrilled inside her heart. She felt his arousal through the material of his pants, and noted it was grossly abundant, and immense. She put her arms around him pulling him closer. The scent of cloves, and something burning wafted into her nostrils.

Then in a fevered fit she pushed him away for it was a public place. His face, wild and flushed, had lost all semblance of the human. She was seeing someone, something else and she became afraid.

"Luc, who are all these people really?"

"I told you, baby, my friends."

"I saw one I knew and he was mafia. Is that what you do Luke?"

"You might say I'm in personnel. No, not strictly mafia, baby.

"Luc, he called you 'The Boss'".

"He was fucking with you, baby. Mafia men like to scare women. I will deal with him."

"Don't hurt him, Luc. He meant no harm. Besides, you don't know who I talked to."

"Lavinia," he said peering into her eyes with a curious expression like a spider to a fly, "I do know. I know everything you do. I've made it my business to know. I really dig you, baby."

"Damn! Then you are mafia!"

"No, baby, not exactly. The underworld, maybe, but not mafia."

"Shit! From bad to worse!" said Lavinia.

"Lavinia, look, I'm not a dealer, hit man, capo, or any of that shit. I'm an advisor, if anything, a businessman. I do not order hits. I advise. I am like that little voice in their heads."

"Shit! Shit! Shit! Now you're telepathic! I can't stand it!"

"Not telepathic, just perceptive, you could say. Stop fighting me, Lavinia! I am going to give you this whole fucking world. Do not, I repeat do not, reject me. This is the first of my many gifts," he said holding out a long, black jeweler's box tied up in silver ribbon.

"Luc, this is only our first date. You don't even know me. How can you give me a gift like this?" she asked.

"I'm giving a gift to the woman I love."

"You're scaring the shit out of me," she said opening the box. Inside was a diamond and emerald necklace.

"Shit, tell me a joke before I freak the hell out!"

"Okay, I'll tell you two. Why is Frosty so popular? Answer. Because he's such a cool guy. Second one. Do you know what is the Tom Jones syndrome? It's not unusual," said Luc.

"They're really bad, Luc."

"I know, but I just like them for some reason. Don't really know why," he replied.

"Luc, give me some time, a week or two. I'm not really clear on men. I just got a divorce a year ago."

"Sure, baby, we have all the time in the world."

THE WEDDING

They left the party and a fine rain was falling, like little, cold bullets of water. Lavinia was feeling light headed and didn't know why. Those probing yellow eyes, and the way he smiled, and the animal grace, so quick he moved. The street lights made rivers of green, yellow, and red reflections in the black asphalt of the road as they waited for a cab. The bar music had died down: it was going on three a.m.

Lavinia became aware of silent footsteps, two men following close behind. One man put his rough hand on Luc's shoulder while the other slid his arm under her neck, muffling her mouth with his other hand. They looked like muggers, everywhere, standard issue. One could expect more drama from things evil but this is not always the case.

"Give us your fucking wallet, SOB, and lady empty your purse into this bag. We don't want no bullshit from you, Mister."

As quick as lightening, Luc disengaged the man from Lavinia, and forcefully put her behind himself. A cab appeared from nowhere and Luc forced her in it, and slammed the door, telling the cabby to take her home. Her protestations for him to come too were ignored. He remained with the two men in horrible freeze frame as the cab pulled away. She wondered why he showed no fear.

Later on, she had a fearful dream. She dreamed a large, gray wolf had attacked the two men and blood was streaming from open wounds at their necks, and coagulated like congealed rubies on the wounds at their chests, and two stray cats were riffling through the trash bins nearby while a rat ran over one of the dead man's sneakers. And Luc was nowhere to be seen. Only the wolf, in horrible deadly detail remained. Not a soul came to help them. Upon arriving home, she had an immediate impulse to call him and see if he were okay but some instinct quelled the impulse. She was afraid to know.

After a week and a half, she began to crave Luc like he was the last Coke on the desert, and she called him. He was delighted and invited her over for dinner. Not a public place, most definitely. They talked of art, and books, and anything they was not really on their minds.

Then after dinner, Luc took her hand, kissed it and said, "It's time we went to bed, Lavinia."

"You're so sure of yourself."

"Uh huh, I am, and I know you want me, too. Let's get it on, honey."

"All right," she replied.

"Baby, I've got to tell you this about myself. I'm going to feel a bit cold at first. Then it's going to feel really, really hot."

"Like Ben Gay."

"No, babe, nothing at all gay I assure you."

So Lavina found herself sprawled out on his black satin sheets like a fucking banquet, or a proud concubine which she was with her legs thrown up in the air and Luc ramming her violently with his powerful cock. He smelled like a rutting goat. Afterward he bruised her pretty lips with the urgency of his kisses and the got up and put on a Tom Jones CD. He purposely put it on 'Delilah' a song about infidelity. The man kills his faithless sweetheart with a knife. And the lyrics are as follows"

'She stood there laughing
And I felt the knife in my hand
And she laughed no more.
Forgive me, Delilah, I just couldn't take anymore.'"

As the lyrics played he put his hand around her neck and stared into her eyes, his black eyes, so moist and passionate, and he said, "You know, darling, I would sure hate to give you reason to be unfaithful." And she arched back and took him again. The itching, pleasantly painful feeling of orgasm did not elude her as she raked his ass with her long, red nails bringing forth blood. They made love all night long in every possible way until the orange rays of the sun filtered through an empty space in his red velvet curtains. She reflected how his bedroom had the appearance of the thirteenth room out of Edgar Allen Poe's prose poem, 'Mask of the Red Death.'

A black servant who looked like a voodoo priestess served them breakfast in bed. For him, it was a mountain of protein, and for her, a simple bowl of vanilla, nonfat yogurt with sliced banana. He explained that he knew she was watching her weight and wanted for her what she wanted for herself. "Beauty is one's poetry to the world, honey," he said.

In the year that followed he made good on all his promises and then some. Their lovemaking was powerful, intense, and sometimes painful for them both. Amazingly, he let her hurt him on occasion. Her pleasure was his pleasure, and vice versa. He understood her as no one ever had, not even Bertie. And she liked his sense of humor, and all his corny jokes, and he prized her wit and creativity. He treated her friends as if they were his family, doing things for them, and solving their problems if need be. The women adored him; the men distrusted, and disliked him. And Luc didn't give a damn: he had his woman.

He came in one day holding a black cat with a diamond collar. However, it wasn't just a black cat: it was actually a tame panther, and he explained that this was the second of his "wedding gifts".

"Are we to be married, Luc?" she asked.

"Of course, love. If you are prescient, you already knew that."

"I did know, and the answer is yes."

"Great, baby, and I'm taking you home with me to my palace. But, Lavinia, there is one little thing you should know about me, hon."

"You're Morman, and I'm the seventh wife. That it?"

"No, nothing that plebian. Something kind of different you might say. About who I really am. Well, here goes, I'm Satan, the devil, and my kingdom is hell. There, I've said it."

"Luc, have you lost your goddamned mind?" she exclaimed.

"Look at me now, baby." Before her stood, the red, horny person, naked as a jay bird, with nine inches of erect, turgid dick.

"Oh, shit, I knew this was too good to be true," she said sadly.

"But it is true, baby. I'm still the man you love, Luc, or Lucifer, if you will. I love the hell out of you, Lavinia."

"Well, it's out of the question. It's just too weird. Besides it's too hot down there and I'd miss my friends, and I'd miss New York. Oh, God!"

"Don't call on him, baby: it's hard enough telling you this. Look at me, I'm erect, and it's all yours. I really dig you, baby. Do not, I repeat, do not reject me. I'm a rich man: I can afford air conditioning, and as for the other, work with me, Lavinia."

"Well, I do love you, Luc. I guess I could do a Persepherone thing. Six months above, six months below."

"Persepherone, Hades, and Demeter. I knew them well. Whatever you want, baby. I agree to anything. I love you, bitch!"

The wedding was set for that Christmas on the twenty fourth because it was Lavinia's favorite holiday, and because Luc always took any opportunity to offend his heavenly Father. They rented an estate in Mount Airy. Luc had initially wanted the wedding to be in Tierra del Fuego (Land of Fire), but Lavinia objected strongly.

"Get it, baby, fire and the devil, like peanut butter and jelly?"

"I'll kick your damn ass, Luc!"

"And you do that so well, baby. All right, it was just a thought. We'll have it around Philadelphia, okay?"

"I don't want my friends to know who you really are. It's bad enough they think you're mafia. And no fucking magic tricks either like going red, and getting naked!"

"I wouldn't, babe. I want to stay in their good graces. Who knows, I may see them in the afterlife."

"You do that, and no ass for an eternity, motherfucker."

"All right, all right. Geez, you're so touchy anymore."

"Do they have sex in heaven, Luc, or is it all harps and angel food cake?"

"Why do you think they call it heaven, baby? All the sex you could want and anchovies on every pizza!"

"No, seriously, Luc."

"Yes, seriously, Lavinia. My Father is a fair man, or spirit, if you will. He gives people whatever they always wanted, whatever that is. The difference in heaven and hell is that in heaven you get any kind of sex you want. In hell, you get the kind of sex you'd never want."

"And, in heaven do they just have a laugh riot every minute?"

"No babe, they have to worship Him, kiss his ass. And there's jobs. He knows people must work. They wouldn't just be happy lying around. There's challenges. People cannot exist without some strife. It's like earth only no utility bills, or foreclosures. But, don't worry, you aint ever going there, babe. Your soul would be completely unacceptable to him. He's a very strict spirit."

"In hell, what's it like for people, Luc?"

"Well, baby, I do enjoy being unpleasant. Nobody gets what they want, they regret who they have been, and there's constant strife. It's kind of like being a mental patient on earth," Luc replied.

"Shit, Luc, you're mean."

"Not to you, baby."

"How can you live with yourself, Luc?"

"Easy, I don't have a conscience, hon, and I like inflicting pain on others, and so do you, baby."

"True, but not always. Not to everyone."

"And it's the same for me. I'm nice to you, aren't I? It's just that I have more responsibilities."

"Well, I guess so, Mr. Prince of Darkness. Who will you invite to the wedding and how many people do you figure on?" asked Lavinia.

"Maybe, one thousand, and I'll invite who the fuck I please. And you do the same."

Lavinia did not argue. The devil is a knucklehead. Everyone knows this. They decided on the color scheme of red and green, an obvious choice and her wedding gown was to be red crepe de chine with a plunging neckline, not so obvious a choice.

"I want every man to envy me. Honey, those little peaches of yours are so beautiful it's just a sin," and he laughed.

There were to be three bands, one of which was The Greatful Dead.

"Let me have this one little joke, honey. Aint nobody glad to be dead especially in hell."

"But Jerry Garcia is dead, Luc."

"And how is this a problem for me, Lavinia?"

"Oh, shit. Ghosts at my wedding!"

"Not ghosts, baby, spirits, or souls. You will like whom I invite."

"What will everyone think?"

"Think I give a flying fuck? This is my show, honey, you got that?"

Again I say the devil is a knucklehead.

The day of the wedding snow fell like ivory flaked inside a paper weight, and Lavinia's heart rose in her chest like a bird in flight. Myrtle and Gladys were so excited for her as was her ex-husband, Bertie. He was a good man who could not fathom evil and did not recognize it if he saw it. Not so for Clive, Gladys' husband, who had checked out Luc's dealings in this earthly sphere. He was afraid for Lavinia, and for the girls. Bertie merely thought his sweet girl was so happy and would never be anything but content, and prosperous. And he was so proud of her creative success as well. Clive thought to himself, "Piss off that bastard, and you are dead!" So, true, so very true, but you would also be in hell with your damn brains boiling in your head, and a constant DVD of your life running every minute!

The priest, a Catholic named Tomas de Torchemada, gave a proper and powerful marriage ceremony. He wore a long purple robe and fallen angels were the flower girls. No one seemed to realize who he was, the lethal and evil Grand Inquisitor of the Spanish Inquisition. No one, that is, but Lavinia. As Bertie gave Lavinia away his face had the transcendent glow of the Christ child himself, and Gladys and Myrtle, her two bridesmaids, were lovely tricked out in their black velvet designer sheaths with really low cut bodices. Luc forbade all pastel colors, saying it reminded him of "goddamned, fucking angels."

"Luc, do you take this woman to be your lawful wedded wife?" intoned the priest in a huge, baritone voice.

"Fuck, yes," replied Luc.

Lavinia laughed and replied in the affirmative as well. And they tongue kissed and grinded a little. and Luc bent her over backwards in a dramatic embrace. They would have humped on the podium except that it was uncomfortable, and people might be shocked. People applauded, and threw petals from black roses as the happy couple passed by. The denizens of hell licked their cracked lips in anticipation of the buffet and well stocked, magnificent bar. A diet of sawdust and sea water could make anyone ravenous for the finer things in life. Yes, indeed!

There were fifteen tables piled high with turkeys, hams, filet mignon, lobsters, crabs, shrimp, and clams and oysters on the half shell. In evidence were the more exotic and foreign delights such as cheeses from all over the world, and game meats like pheasant, wild duck, and elk. The salad tables were monstrous in their variety and color with the avocado, Lavinia's favorite food, being a featured item. Exotic cakes and pies were in evidence, and many flavors of ice cream including that old favorite, Rocky Road. Luc got this flavor especially ordered to remind people of their trials and tribulations in life. He didn't care if they perceived his wit and cruelty.

Luc took the microphone in hand on the dance floor and made the following announcement."

"Everyone, eat until you pop, and don't' consider leaving here sober! Mi casa, tu casa. And dancing's on the main floor and the second floor. Dance your asses off, and may all the ladies, seventy and older, please come have a dance with me. I am your long lost son. If anyone isn't having a good time please tell your old Uncle Luc and I'll order up a miracle! This is the happiest day of my long and profligate life. Thanks for being with me! I love you!"

And Luc glowed with a warm yellow light like a very angel, which he was. They cut the forty foot wedding cake (devil's food) at midnight and dispensed pieces to most everyone. On top of each piece was a giant dollop of Rocky Road ice cream. After the reception was over, Lavinia mentioned she was not happy at having Hitler, Mussolini, and Emperor Hiro Hito at her wedding.

"Oh, what do you want, babe? They're the Axis of Evil. And they're my buddies. I torture their asses all the time. I just figured I'd let them out for a while. Where's your Christmas spirit, honey?"

"And Torchemada, why was he our priest? Couldn't you have gotten someone else, goddamnit?"

"Well, honey, he was available, and he was free. I spent fucking two mil on this wedding!"

"And I'm not worth it, cocksucker?"

"You are, definitely, baby, and I do not suck cock, hon."

"My friends were freaked. If they weren't so drunk I would not have been able to convince them those were just actors! I told them you just had a weird sense of humor! You embarrass me, Luc!"

"How about I bare ass you?" And he unzipped his pants revealing a raging hard-on. "Better yet, get down on your knees, bitch, and give me some mouth action right this very minute!"

And she did as told. He was the only man who could ever command her. Afterward, in as moment of weakness, she admitted she didn't mind Oppenheimer, the scientist, in so much as he was an intellectual and a great conversationalist. Oppenheimer, of course as it is known, invented the atomic bomb, the first man to split a cell, and make it go boom! Later on, she expressed some reservations about spending time in hell.

"What will I do in hell, Luc, while you work?"

"Same thing you do up here. Write, go to parties, socialize, eat, drink, You know, the whole kit and caboodle. There are some very interesting people in hell, baby. You make like them when they're not bitching and moaning. It seems I do pick on them, poor things."

"Like who? Who will I find interesting, Luc?"

"Come with me, and see, hon. I've even got a job for you. That is, when you're not writing."

"What, may I ask?"

"I'm putting you in charge of the S&M division. You'll torture the sadists and be excruciatingly kind to the masochists. It's perfect for you, baby."

Lavinia screamed, then burst out in laughter.

"Luc, you're such a son of a bitch! That's why I love you so! I like it! I like it very much. I can just see me with the Marquise de Sade.

'Marquise, I'm going to do to you everything you ever did to any woman. What's good for the goose is good for the gander'. And with Hitler, Caligula, and fucked up serial killers like Ed Gein, I'll say, 'Hello, boys. I'm your new boss. Bend over and spread em. Open wide for your old mama!' This is a fucking scream, Luc. I love it! And when the masochists ask me to whip them or shit like that, I'll say, 'I couldn't possibly do that, darling. I just love you so much!"

So ends my tale of our winsome three, and they do wish you well. Except for Lavinia. Pray tell. It's best to stay out of hell, gentle reader.